May Hill

Robert Wexelblatt

ISBN: 978-93-6354-240-2

First Edition: 2024
Rs. 200/-

Cyberwit.net
HIG 45 Kaushambi Kunj, Kalindipuram
Allahabad - 211011 (U.P.) India
http://www.cyberwit.net
Tel: +(91) 9415091004
E-mail: info@cyberwit.net

Printed at Repro India Limited.

Acknowledgments

"May Hill" and "Mrs. Podolski on Forgiveness" first appeared in *Offcourse Literary Journal*

"Schrader's Misdemeanor" first appeared in *Forge Literary Journal*

"Petite Suite de Musées" and "The Ex-Consul" first appeared in *BlazeVOX*

"Le Parlement des Amis Imaginaires" first appeared in *Heartland Review*

"Petite Suite non Résolue" first appeared in *Amarillo Bay*

"Petite Suite de Musiciens" first appeared in *Punt Volat*

"Inside the Pale" first appeared in *Infinity Wanderers*

"Dying Amandato" first appeared in *The Monocacy Valley Review*

"Ein Heldenleben" first appeared in *Talking River Review*

"Mrs. Podolski Defines Schlimmbesserung" first appeared in *Eyeshot Literary Magazine*

"The End of the War" first appeared in *Cleaver Magazine*

Cover Illustration: Photograph of May Hill, Gloucestershire

Source: Wikimedia Commons

Contents

May Hill

When Sarah Sala was eleven years old her parents took her to the Cheltenham Festival in Gloucestershire. Though it was March, damp and chilly, Sarah insisted that they climb May Hill. Her mother, who felt a cold coming on and wanted to attend a piano recital, declined, but her well-read father was all for it. As they began the ascent, he recited a verse from Ivor Gurney: *May Hill that Gloucester dwellers 'gainst every sunset see.* Sarah said she liked the rhythm but there was something odd about it. Her scholarly father, a lecturer in Romance Languages, had the knack of being droll and pedantic at once. He told Sarah the oddity was because of Gurney's outlandish sentence structure. "It's Teutonic because you have to wait so long for the verb." His own family was Italian, not German. Sarah's Sala grandparents had emigrated from Milan before the war. Her other grandparents, the Jewish Blumfelds, were also an immigrant family. They arrived two generations before the Salas. As for Sarah's parents, both were thoroughly English, right down to their inoffensive agnosticism, but Sarah may have been the most English of all.

When she was little, Sarah often asked to hear the story of how her parents met. She liked hearing both her parents' versions. They agreed that their relationship began by a lucky mischance in the Michaelhouse Café where the undergraduate who would become Sarah's mother stumbled in her haste to join some friends and spilled hot tea over the graduate student who would become her father. His version emphasized the temperature of the tea and the brand-newness of his herringbone Harris tweed. Sarah's mother's version was more amusing because she used the story to explain the distinction between *schlemiel* and *schlimazel.* "*I* was the schlemiel," she would say at the end of the story then wait for Sarah's jubilant response: "And *dad* was the *schlimazel*!"

Sarah's mother was a talented pianist who offered lessons to the children of Cambridge. She began Sarah on the instrument when she was barely three. It quickly became obvious that Sarah was a prodigy. She had perfect pitch, played beautifully, and was a whiz at sight-reading. Moreover, her appetite for music was insatiable. Her favorite thing to do was to lie on the carpet, drawing pictures and listening to her mother's collection of vinyl disks and CDs. One rainy afternoon, her mother played her Jacqueline du Pré's recording of Elgar's *Cello Concerto* and told the story of the cellist's life and early death. Like Sarah, du Pré was English but had a foreign name. She thought du Pré glamorously tragic, a romantic heroine, a worthy idol. Sarah's instrument would not be the piano.

Sarah's Englishness was rooted in the Cambridgeshire countryside of her childhood and her visits to London concert halls, both of which were embodied in the music she loved best, the string compositions of Holst, Butterworth, Parry, Bridge, Britten, and Vaughn-Williams. In her teens she conceived a particular affection for the instrumental works of Gerald Finzi who, like du Pré, suffered an early death. She shared with him a Jewish background and an Italian surname and thought him unjustly neglected. When she learned from a biography that Finzi's ashes were scattered on May Hill she was deeply moved. She remembered climbing the hill and it deepened her bond. When she was asked what she wanted for her fifteenth birthday, Sarah begged for another trip to Gloucestershire to climb May Hill again. She told her parents she wanted to pay homage to Gerald Finzi.

Sarah attended the Netherhall School and studied cello privately, first with Helen Knox-Thompson and then Nigel Threlkeld. Her father arranged for her to audit two music history classes at the University. She was happy almost all the time.

Then, suddenly and to Sarah's horror, everything went topsy-turvy. Her father received an offer of a professorship from the University of Pennsylvania with a good prospect of tenure. Sarah's whining objections felt selfish and flimsy, even to her. Her mother told her about Philadelphia's excellent Curtis Institute of Music and said she was confident Sarah would be accepted there with a letter from Threlkeld and a successful audition. And that is what happened. Sarah took some solace in the high praise of the Institute's panel.

The family settled in the suburb of Cheltenham, chosen for its Gloucestershire name, which somewhat appeased Sarah. That it reportedly had many Jewish residents made her mother, appalled by the brutal rhetoric of America's politics and the violence of its films, feel safer. After a quick adjustment and a good year, Sarah's parents decided that they would stay and become citizens. Her father said jovially they would make it a family event. "In four years, we can submit our N-400 forms together, in a bunch." Sarah bridled until her father explained dual citizenship, that being American didn't mean she had to give up being English.

Sarah excelled at Curtis and was soon performing regularly with the Institute's chamber groups. Her father arranged for her and her mother to play three of Beethoven's cello sonatas at the University, and Sarah was asked back to perform three of Bach's suites.

Sarah's sentimental education was limited but instructive. Some boys were drawn to her seriousness, others captivated when she said things like different *to* and not different *from*. She liked the idea of appearing exotic, like the vivacious oboist from Brazil and the morose violinist from Croatia. Then she figured out it was something a little different. When she spoke up in class, everyone quieted down and paid attention, even the teacher, just because of her pronunciation. She amused her parents by observing that the American Revolution had done away with British rule but evidently not the colonial authority of an Oxbridge accent.

Though her adolescence was hardly a social whirlwind, it was not without heartbreak. Like any other school seething with teenagers, Curtis was a hormonal hothouse. Sarah had one serious romance. She even cultivated two girlfriends just to talk to them about Randolph, a brilliant composition student two years ahead of her. Randolph was intense in how he looked and spoke, in all he did. He had broad tastes. He idolized Alban Berg but admired Francis Poulenc. He talked fast, speed-read Mann, Dostoyevsky, and Unamuno. It was as if he was always facing a deadline. Randolph too was charmed by her accent, but he was also attracted by a seriousness that matched his own. Then he graduated and secured a scholarship to study in Paris. He phoned Sarah three times, texted four, and that was that. The tatters of her old Cambridge accent couldn't compete with a fresh French one. "C'est la vie," she said to her worried mother. And then she graduated, too.

At twenty, Sarah's future was uncertain. No manager stepped forward; however, a retirement opened a position in the Philadelphia Orchestra, and her teachers at Curtis encouraged her to apply. Sarah was keen though feared it might be overreaching. Her parents weren't encouraging because of her age. Not wanting her to build her hopes too high, her father shared some research.

"The average age of an orchestra member in this country is forty-six. It's even older in Europe."

Her mother was gentler but even more anxious, afraid that her only child, who had known nothing but success, might be crushed. But thanks to the influence of Curtis, Sarah was granted an audition. Despite their doubts, her parents rented her a better cello. She chose Bach's *Sixth Suite* and practiced like mad on the new instrument.

Sarah's father asked her how she liked the fancy cello.

"Like it? It's how I imagine driving a Bentley would feel. Thank you, thank you, thank you, Papa. *Grazie mille volte*!"

The panel was impressed. One member, the concert master, asked if she felt prepared to play something more. She smiled, nodded, took a deep breath, and played the *Forlana* from Finzi's *Five Bagatelles* in her own arrangement. It was the Finzi, she believed, that closed the deal. When the phone call with the good news came that she would be offered a one-year probationary contract, Sarah only grinned at her parents, not out of arrogance, but to keep herself from jumping up and down and screaming *I told you so*.

Sarah was not only a rookie but of a different generation from her colleagues. Many were charmed and supportive, but quite a few were neither. The latter were pleased when a visiting conductor, a notorious tyrant, halted a rehearsal to correct her timing. The stickler corrected several other players too but Sarah felt humiliated and was out of sorts for a week. She buckled down, mastered her parts, paid strict attention to tempi and, in general, was a good soldier. As she said to her father, "I keep my knees apart and my head down." At the end of the season, the orchestra's music director asked to see her privately and told her what a good job she had done. Even if it was patronizing, Sarah was nonetheless pleased. It meant that she wasn't being let go.

When the schedule for the next season was announced, Sarah was thrilled. A renowned Swedish soloist, a man whose playing she admired, had asked to make a change in the program. Instead of the Dvorak concerto, he wanted to play Gerald Finzi's. The conductor explained to his troops.

"Mr. Bengtsson thinks the Finzi concerto is an underappreciated masterpiece and far too infrequently performed. I asked Fred to check and, sure enough, our orchestra has never performed the Finzi. In a sense, it will be a premiere for the audience, especially our subscribers, all of whom already know the Dvorak. My point? We've all got important work to do before our guest arrives for rehearsals. And, by the way, I think he's right about the Finzi."

Bengtsson was tall, even for a Swede, not blond but with a straight, dignified posture and a handsome if rather narrow face. His salt-and-pepper hair was close-cropped. He reminded Sarah a little of Max von Sydow in *The Seventh Seal*. She found him livelier than his photographs suggested; that is, when he was playing. When he was not, he appeared as distant and cold as a fjord. He played well, but in Sarah's view with more correctness than feeling. But this was just in rehearsal when restraint is to be expected. The performance was yet to come.

But then it didn't. It seemed Bengtsson had eaten something he shouldn't or had picked up a stomach bug. The day before the first of the three scheduled concerts, he cancelled. Like everybody, the conductor was disappointed, though not so sorely as Sarah. He said they would be substituting Mozart's *Prague Symphony* which they had performed that summer for the traditional free concert at the Mann Center. He added that a few of the subscribers might be unhappy, but in his opinion most would be content to swap unfamiliar Finzi for tried-and-true Mozart.

Sarah didn't give what she did after this speech any thought at all. Raising her hand with the bow in it, she turned herself into a human exclamation point.

"I can play the Finzi. I love the concerto. I know it by heart, Maestro."

There was a moment of shock, then derisive whispering followed by some barely muffled laughter. Sarah heard a word her mother sometimes used disapprovingly, *chutzpah.* The conductor just stared at her.

In the ardent grip of her idea, Sarah began to play the *Andante Quieto* and, slowly, quiet spread from the strings to the woodwinds, to the brass, and all the way to the percussionists.

The A-minor *Cello Concerto*, Opus 40, was Gerald Finzi's last significant work. It was commissioned for the 1955 Cheltenham Festival. Finzi had been diagnosed with untreatable Hodgkin's disease four years earlier and given up to ten years to live. He got only half of that, dying fourteen months after his concerto's premiere. To Sarah, the concerto conveyed many meanings, but one of these was a farewell to music and to life, *ein Abschied.* To her, the cello was an autobiographical character. In effect, it bore the soul of Gerald Finzi.

With only two days to prepare, Sarah lacked the time to think of anything but the concerto, to master the score and reassure her conductor. She ignored her parents and thought only of Finzi and the music's meaning, how it expressed his love of his wife Joy and of rural England but also his despair. Listening is done from the outside, performing from the inside. She thought of Finzi's need to get away from his native London to the countryside, though it was in the city that he made his career, his marriage, and his best friends. Finzi composed the concerto in Gloucestershire, home to Cheltenham—the *real* one, Sarah couldn't help thinking—within sight of May Hill.

As always, Finzi wrote lyrically, even in the roiling first movement. He gives the cello an extended cadenza that slowly mourns and soars but is no virtuosic showpiece. He makes the cello sing like an alto with a three-octave range. In the end, though, the ominous tones of the orchestra bludgeon the singer into silence.

As she performed in the first concert, Sarah's heart swelled. She played better than she ever had before, better than Bengtsson had, especially in the *andante quieto*, her favorite movement, to her, the quintessence of the composer. It is lovely, peaceful, romantic. Sarah filled it with her own nostalgia and longing, with the ineradicable Englishness she felt she shared with Finzi. When she closed her eyes she pictured the green countryside, the narrow lanes, and the swell of May Hill. When the movement ended, some in the audience began to applaud, which isn't supposed to happen. Then others joined in. The conductor turned around and, with a broad and sympathetic smile to the hall, gently motioned for quiet.

Sarah played the last movement in an altered state imagining the spirits of Finzi and du Pré standing on either side of her. When it was over, the audience stood and cheered. A triumph.

The headline of the *Inquirer's* review read "A Star is Born." During the following week there were requests for interviews, including one from a network morning show. The Sunday *Times* ran an article with her graduation snapshot from Curtis. A management company called. There were invitations to perform the Finzi concerto from Cleveland and San Francisco. Both conductors phoned personally, and one flattered Sarah by saying she might be to Finzi what du Pré was to Elgar. Teachers from the Institute sent flowers, and the Director asked her to consider a part-time position working with the younger students and, of course, the cellists.

Her parents rejoiced for her, but they did so discreetly and offered no advice. The exaltation lasted hardly more than a week, worn away by all the attention and too many options. Alone late in the night, Sarah gave herself up to the compelling nostalgia she had felt while playing the concerto. She felt Finzi's longing for the country, his displacement. On an impulse, she contacted the Cheltenham Symphony, also the Newent and Gloucestershire orchestras, all semi-professional. She sent an inquiry about a teaching post to the Gloucestershire Academy of Music. Then, raising her sights, she wrote formally to the City of Birmingham Symphony, the Hallé Orchestra, and the London Philharmonic. Even without a secure position, Sarah was determined to move back to England.

It took her parents some time to absorb and process the shock of their daughter's decision. They were surprised by her rejection of so many opportunities, perhaps disappointed, already missing her. Her mother especially needed time to ease her way to resignation. But it seemed like acquiescence when she prepared a traditional Sunday dinner of roast beef, Britishly overdone, with sprouts and Yorkshire pudding. Little was said about Sarah's choice, but over the apple crumble her father began to reminisce about their trips to May Hill. It was typical of him to make it literary. He wistfully quoted two lines from Masefield.

I've marked the May Hill ploughman stay

There on his hill, day after day.

"Is that it?" he asked rather shrewdly.

"Yes. In part. Don't, please, get me wrong. It's been good here, *very* good, but I want to go home."

"Home?" said her mother sharply. "Isn't *this* home?"

"I'm sorry, Mum. That came out wrong."

Her mother picked up the plates and vanished into the kitchen maybe to wash, maybe to weep.

Sarah's father grimaced and motioned Sarah toward the living room. They sat opposite each other.

He posed a few practical questions, all of which Sarah answered rather vaguely. Then Professor Sala, master of the lingua franca of literature, asked her whether she knew Robert Frost's poem "The Road Not Taken."

"I don't think anybody in Philadelphia gets out of high school without reading it, Dad."

"Really? Well, yes, that's good. Do you happen to know where Frost wrote it and why?"

"Nope, but I expect you're going to tell me."

Her father took a deep breath and spoke softly. "Frost lived in England from 1912 to 1915. One of the friends he made there was the writer, Edward Thomas. The two liked taking walks together. One day they happened on two roads. Thomas couldn't decide which they should take and later mentioned to Frost that he regretted not taking the one they didn't. Shortly after, Frost returned to New Hampshire and sent Thomas a copy of the poem that everybody in Philadelphia has to read in high school. Some think it was Frost's poem that led Thomas to enlist. He was killed two years later, in Arras, just after being sent to the Front.

"No, I didn't know all that. Where did Frost live in England? Where did he and Thomas take that walk with the two roads?"

"In Gloucestershire, my dear."

Sarah sighed then smiled. "So, maybe the road they took led to the top of May Hill?"

"Maybe. Or perhaps it didn't."

Schrader's Misdemeanor

The courthouse looked like a new elementary school and had a funny odor too, nearly as I could tell a sort of mixture of acrylic carpeting and french fries. The lighting was wrong, muted fluorescent bulbs of the kind favored by shopping malls. Accustomed to the pillared piles of the North I couldn't help feeling the place lacked a certain dignity, not unlike me.

Though guilty is pretty much what I've been pleading since puberty, I'd never actually done it in a court of law. Imagine my anticipation, the sleepless night, how I pictured myself standing before the Law. The actuality proved a disappointment, though not a bitter one. If you're a delinquent, have violated the mores of the tribe, you have a right to expect a show, an impressive philippic from the prosecutor or a screed from the bench, at the very least an opportunity to bow your head in token of remorse. In fact, marring my immaculate criminal record of sixty-six years was no more bother than getting a haircut—less, a haircut can take half an hour.

Hustled in by Kinderman, the thirtyish lawyer Sheila selected from the *Yellow Pages* when she decided to update our wills, charged by the bailiff, a scrawny fellow with a pair of handcuffs hanging from the back of his belt, asked for a plea by the uninterested judge, I delivered myself of one contrary Kinderman's advice. The judge said *fine*, knocked his wooden hammer, and pfft, we were out of there. Outside, a second court officer, also underweight, put his hand on my shoulder and pointed me down the corridor. I went into a small office where I wrote a check for a hundred and seventy-five dollars, the sum of my debt to society, and handed it over to a lady with fussily styled hair and an accent from the heart of Dixie. She was even more polite than the bailiffs, smiling and issuing me a florid receipt written with a fountain pen charged with peacock blue ink. "Thank you . . . Mr. Schrader," she said, thoughtfully examining my check in order to call me by name. So, I paid up and that was it, more or less; shorn and shriven. The overall impression was that I was more customer than criminal. When I came out Kinderman, who had been laying for me in the hall, slapped me on the back, shook his head, and said he really believed he could've gotten me off. On the steps outside he mentioned he'd send me his bill. I didn't ask what for.

It was only ten-thirty, but the parking lot was already hot as Hades. At the side entrance three chained black prisoners stood sweating beside a police van. I tried to feel like them. They were not customers, not in orange overalls, not in manacles.

From across the sun-blanched asphalt, Detective Freyling, my arresting officer and sole witness for the prosecution, threw me an affectionate wave and wagged his finger in an avuncular fashion, then climbed into his grey, unmarked Ford. You could tell by the way he drew his long legs up he was a Clint Eastwood fan.

The parking lot was bordered on one side by four so-called Royal palms, primitive, Dr. Seussish trees. Sheila loved them, saw them forming the foreground of romantic sunsets; but, whenever she waxed poetic about the things, I'd say that palm trees evolved for giant lizards to rub their scales against, not the dry skin of retired college administrators. It was Sheila's idea to move down here. First, there were the vacations, then a sabbatical semester, and, finally, lock, stock, and the two bookcases she allowed me. Here in Elderland you can forget about playing old for the young, which is okay; still, there are times when I'm revolted, when I'm overwhelmed by the conviction that Florida, as my grandson Jason succinctly puts his negative appraisals, sucks. With Jason, things are either awesome or they suck. Well, I had one of these suckish moments in the parking lot of the courthouse. Parking lots are terrible spaces, open invitations to forgetfulness and agoraphobia, not to mention violence and death. I cheered myself up with the thought that, though I'd missed the freedom rides and voter registration drives of the sixties, at least I'd managed to get myself busted down South once before I kicked the bucket.

I'd been able to keep Julie McAllister and Ellen Hacker out of the business only because Detective Freyling was a relatively good sort, at least to old white men and white women. I remember how he was waiting for us at the dock, one foot picturesquely up on his unmarked Ford's fender, how he drew me aside, explained the nature of my transgression, and offered not to charge Julie if I didn't give him a hard time. I have to admit that I like his assuming gallantry on my part. We shook on it. Then he said I should follow him down to the station for the paperwork.

A little swearing from Julie in the background as we drove off. But no handcuffs. No fingerprinting. No speech about my right to remain silent.

Guilty, I'd said. *I plead guilty, Your Honor.* It came out smoothly, far more easily than saying my own name. Being one of those atheists who believe in original sin, I'd spent my whole life red-handed, so to speak. A dutiful husband, Your Honor, but nevertheless an evildoer, a polluter of the seas, if that's how you insist on looking at it.

I had to laugh at the irony. I'd been arrested for carrying out Sheila's last wish and she was always such a stickler about the law. All those years she did our taxes I couldn't once convince her to cheat even a dime's worth. A respecter of parking meters and speed limits was Sheila, fastidious about all the ways people like us come into contact with the Rules. She didn't know this one though and, of course, ignorance of the law is no excuse.

Freyling and I had met a year before and that was because of Sheila too. I had been selfishly off on my morning bike ride when the stroke crumpled her in the Winn Dixie parking lot so that, when, two days later, I got a call from a detective, I thought for a moment I might be under arrest for allowing an unaccompanied woman with hypertension to buy chicken. Freyling offered condolences and told me he was holding Sheila's wedding ring for me. Hadn't I noticed it was missing? No, of course he understood why I wouldn't have noticed. A great shock, of course, a terrible shock. He was very sorry. He explained about the ring in his tough, solicitous voice in which there remained a soupçon of Jersey. I had the idea that he was pleased with himself, that he considered this a sweet part of the job. "The EMS guys are trained to remove all jewelry before they drop people at the hospital. I'm afraid, you know, the orderlies . . . Did you get your wife's wallet back? They needed that for the insurance card and I.D. Yes? Good. Anyway, Mr. Schrader, the ring's here waiting for you. I've got it right here in an envelope with your name on it. Come by any time. Just give your name at the desk and mention mine. Detective Freyling. F-R-E-Y-*ling*."

Eleven months later he busted me, just happened to be gazing out at Julie's boat in the bay that morning and somehow figured out what we were up to. He was shrewd, kind, brave, bigoted, and fond of telling war stories. When I went to pick up Sheila's ring, he had a fresh one. "It happened outside the Winn Dixie, didn't it?" he said, meaning the death of my wife. "Well, this colleague of mine was down in that exact same parking lot just last week—you know, shopping with the wife." Was this a reproach, an accusation? "About eight-thirty, you know, just getting dark, and this doped-up dickhead pops out from behind a van and pulls a knife on his wife." Freyling was grinning. "My pal was a little behind with another cart. He could see the kid was nervous, and that's always dangerous. 'Okay, bitch, the money,' says the jerk. Joe ditches his cart, dashes around the car, and steps in front of his wife." Freyling leaned forward menacingly and broke into dialect, waving an upturned fist as if he held a knife in it. "'You gonna be a hero, m'fuck?'" Freyling paused, maybe to let the suspense build, maybe to make sure I knew that deep down I shared his anger and fear, his hatred of young African-American males, even making a face to show how certain he was of it. Then he picked up a pencil. "You know there're some civilians want to make it, so we're not allowed to pack our Glocks when we're off duty. Yeah, *real* smart idea. Anyway, my friend pulls out his nine-millimeter and puts one through the bastard's head. Kapow!" Freyling pointed with the pencil just above the parabola formed by his two well defined eyebrows. Then he leaned back for a little politicking. "It's a public safety issue, Mr. Schrader. A police officer isn't ever entirely off duty. In fact, that's how I retrieved your late wife's ring. The ambulance guys gave me a call at home."

It's risky to break the law if you're black. Your retired white folk in air-conditioned Hondas, on the other hand, look like victims, smell like prey, make good customers.

White folk live in they birthday cake houses next the ocean. You can hear they air conditioners hum like a choir, windows never open. They big white cars. They clothes, they smooth white boats. Lie all over theys beaches gettin dark, gettin cancer. Black folk squat in tarpaper shacks, no windowglass, four blocks in. And in. And in till you get to where not even gators'll go the air so mossy marshy you think you drowinin if you yawn up wide. Forgive him his trespasses, Auntie Pearl used to say, puttin her hand on my head, draggin me off to church. You go over that line what you think goin happen to you? It's like you dyin of thirst and they dangle this big drippin glass of lemonade in front of you all cool and wet and say, now just you dare touch it, sip it, slurp it down. You see the lemonade on the TV and then you see them drivin by in they lemonade cars, shrivelled up little white ladies lookin scared and even worse the flashy pink lemonade men with they music boomin and all. Blue done dared me. He did. Just last week he done knocked over some lady and got him fifteen dollars and we bought beer and when we drunk three each, he dared me, called me pussy, called me rev'rend cause I didn't want to go stickin no knife in nobody's face for no fifteen dollars, even gave me his own knife. Auntie coughin, Jasmine sayin candy, candy and Uncle Billy moanin and limpin round so's he can't work no more, not like theys work he's not up to doin. What I'd like is to get up north like maybe this knife of Blue's cut me a path to Detroit or even New York. Yeah, I'd've dared my way through all the white ladies in the world but I don't want to slice nobody and I real scared and I need to scare the shit out of this big ugly white man; who'd've thought he got a gun just my damn luck but surprise or no surprise don't mind much neither, cause maybe up north ain't even really up north while dead is dead anywhere.

We were having drinks on the terrace. Teresa had been nearly jolly greeting us at the door. She looked good too, nice tan set off by a turquoise and hot pink sundress, robust tennis calves. The conversation meandered from movies to the hare-brained environmentalists' proposal to rip out the Australian pines to make space for the hideous indigenous weeds. It was Sheila who brought up the indigenosity issue. She happened to be partial to those pines, lovely non-palms that look like the cloudy evergreens in Chinese watercolors, and she asked Teresa if she'd join an organization she was thinking of putting together, a pro-Aussie-pine league. Teresa bravely said she would and even kept up with the battle plan until, after her second whiskey sour, she started to fall apart. Al tried to cover, ratcheting up his crude humor with a story about some shenanigans on the semi-nude beach, but Teresa's mood sunk us all in a tar pit out of which even big Al's reptilian jokes couldn't climb. "What's the mat—" Sheila began, then guessed. "Oh, Tree. You went to the doctor today."

Teresa spilled it all. It was supposed to be just a routine check-up, some poking, drop of blood, then off for two sets of doubles. But the doctor made them wait and when he emerged from whatever he was doing in back he looked grim. Apparently, they hadn't gotten it all. *It.* "What an idiot I was not to have the whole damned thing off—both of them. Boobs . . . *boobs kill!"* She began to sob. Sheila sprang over and kneeled down beside the chaise and hugged Teresa, buried herself between those ample, fatal bosoms. They were both crying. Al looked at me stricken and for a moment I thought I ought to go over and hug him too. But I did nothing.

The sky looked like an upturned bowl of mother-of-pearl the sun was rolling down. Teresa talked out the medical possibilities while Al added a few hollow optimisms as he barbecued shrimp which we subsequently didn't touch. After coffee, Al suggested he and I go for a walk. "Let's leave them alone with each other," he whispered. Al needed to get out. We ambled down to the golf course, and I let him talk until he didn't want to talk any more. I felt lucky. I felt as if I had managed things better.

Sheila and I went home early, around eight-thirty. She was wrung out and I couldn't think of anything to say. Tree was her best pal in all of Florida. Before we went inside, she pointed out toward the bay and made me promise that, if she should go first, I would have her cremated and scatter her ashes over the water, right there. "You know how I love it, how I love to swim. Fire and water are clean. The very idea of the boneyard's always made me sick. Rotting, the worms, not to mention the ridiculous waste of money and space. People going and looking at a pile of dirt. And while I'm at it, no funeral either, dear. Ghastly things." Owing to the occasion, it wasn't the sort of request you could laugh off. I gave my wife my word, silently assuring myself, as husbands do, that I'd be the first to check out.

I can't remember a time when Sheila didn't overshadow me, order me around, all for my own good, of course. I hated her for it when we were kids, rebelled against her when I grew strong enough, tried to ignore her when I married Paul, but all the while I was leaning on her and never knew it. She was my big sister and she loved to pull rank. To tell the truth, as soon as the shock of her death let up, I felt relieved. It's a terrible thing to have to be ashamed of your own feelings, but there it was. I felt it was a liberation; I was on my own at last. When she went off to college I moved into her room and changed everything around and kept at Pop until he bought me that new bed. I hated sleeping in hers. I tried to fight her loads of times. Like when we put Mom in the nursing home and she worked out the finances, insisting on using up the whole estate before Medicare kicked in. She was always right, always the level-headed one, the honest one. Brighter, taller, better hair. When I fell on my skates, when nobody asked me out, when I had a bad period, when I didn't know what else to do, it wasn't Mom or Pop I ran to, but Sheila.

My sister-in-law Millie was never what you'd call comfortable with me. It was as if she suspected me of something, sensed my guiltiness wasn't merely the disarming, neurotic dodge people usually took it for. Sheila and I didn't see her and Paul all that often, just the occasional holiday, except for the awful time when my mother-in-law had to go into the nursing home. Paul and I got on all right. Whenever they came over, the women would wrangle about the arrangements. I'd give him a beer; we'd talk American league and movies in the den. Paul taught high school kids U.S. history, but his real passion was coaching baseball. In middle age, Millie started up a little antique business. Sheila was proud of her, but Millie resented even Sheila's approval. Then I retired and we moved down here, and we hardly saw them at all, only phone calls.

Neither funeral nor burial. You just telephoned; it was something like ordering from L. L. Bean. They take all major credit cards and everything is neat and clean, just as Sheila wanted. Then they asked me, "Will you be wanting the ashes, sir?" I remembered my promise and said yes. They came Federal Express, brown paper around a wooden box, not even an urn. I didn't unwrap it. Who knows? Maybe the wood was Australian pine. I knew what I was supposed to do but I couldn't part with them, not yet. Sheila was wrong about funerals. Mourners need the ritual not to dwell on their losses but to finish with them. The night she died I called Jill and George and Millie. I wanted something from each of them, but I didn't know what. The consolation of shared pain? A family? Whatever it was I didn't get it. And when I told Millie there wouldn't be any funeral, she didn't seem surprised or upset. When I said something silly about needing a ritual to say goodbye, she hesitated then suggested a memorial service. "A little thing, just for the family." She even offered her home because the kids lived nearer to her than to me. "Besides," she said, "you know how Paul hates traveling." And so, when I took the plane north, I had Sheila's ashes with me, wrapped up in brown paper and labeled, just as they were Fedexed from the crematorium.

"What the hell is *that*?" Millie said when I showed her the package.

"The ashes."

"Sheila's *ashes*?" She turned to Paul and whispered too loudly, "Jesus. Unbelievable."

The service was not quite a fiasco, but near enough. Once again I was disappointed. Millie brought out a couple of photo albums. We all stared at them, turned the pages in silence. George and Allison glared at me as usual, and Jill looked sullen. Jason didn't know what to do with himself and kept bumping into fragile antiques. Millie kept looking hard at me. I spoke, but badly. To tell the truth, I broke down and didn't get very far. Then George spoke. He was suave, eloquent too, though in a bitter sort of way. Jill declined to say anything at all; she just shook her head. Paul put his arm around my shoulders, his big coach's arm, and I felt like a pitcher who'd just given up a winning grand slam.

The grievance against fathers is one of the données, one of the clichés of the twentieth century, or was until recently. It looks as if the Oedipus thing got banged up in the inflation of the seventies and then Reagan gave it the coup de grâce. My students are all into ancestor worship, a whole generation of exceptions demolishing a rule. What this means, of course, is that my own anger is not archetypal but historical, not instinctual but personal. I can remember the class exactly. I was lecturing on the uprisings of 1848 and wanted the kids, who weren't all that much younger than I was, to relate. It was just a few years too late to draw the analogy to 1968, historical amnesia having already entered its golden age, and so I dropped some glib line about the eternal conflict between the generations. Massinger, one of the brightest, raised his hand to say (openly! in front of his peers!) that his father was his model, hero, ideal, just what he aspired to become. I was stunned. Others chimed in. The young women all claimed to adore their mothers as well as their fathers. If there'd been a window in 505 Winslow Hall Freud would have flown out of it. And Gide and Kafka and Nietzsche and the rest of the boys. Just a big pendulum swing? terror of falling out of the middle class? anti-idealism? desperate clutching at the tatters of the thermonuclear family? At that instant I felt myself outdated, decisively alienated from all these Stepford children. Curiously, I also felt younger than my sophomores and a little envious of them, as though they had already achieved a maturity that eluded me and put behind the resentments of their sixteenth year (I refuse to believe they never felt them) while I still couldn't be in a room with my father for half an hour without challenging him, taking offense, mucking things up. Now I look for signs in Jason to see which way he'll go. Will the pendulum of history ever bring us to 1848 again? to 1968? Allison believes it's that my parents never accepted her. Accepted yes, loved no. Nobody ever got over that first Thanksgiving when she forgot to defrost the turkey and there were all those snide comments about neatness, dirt, disorder. True, Allison never charmed Dad and maybe charm and fertility are the chief virtues one looks for in a daughter-in-law. Or does there have to be some unmentionable sexual spark as well? But the rancor goes deeper, back further. To what? I can't even remember. Whatever image I catch at makes me think there's a preceding one. And Mother acting like the moderator in a reactor, "Can't you two talk more quietly?" she'd say. "We're discussing, which is quiet arguing," he'd insist as if it were all a joke, as though it was nothing to argue with a son his humor always belittled. Yet I became an academic, identifying to that extent with the enemy, albeit I mistrust all administrators, daddies every one, shoving the talent around like sheep. When Mother died suddenly like that, nothing lingering that you could get used to, but quick the way she did everything she'd made up her mind to, I was thrown for a loop, went on talking to her in my head for weeks, hearing her voice calling my name when I raked leaves. I went to phone her every Sunday morning, having to stop and remember only he would answer and that no matter what we said we'd both be talking about her absence. Was that it? Were we always fighting over her? Was her death a judgment on us both? If I'd had to choose a parent to stick around there'd be no contest but since he's still here I'm going to make damn sure he sees how different it is between me and Jason, no shaming jokes, no contests, just to prove somebody really can learn from history.

The kids all left after the memorial service. George, Allison, and Jason crammed into their Toyota, Allison tight-lipped with her colorless milk-fed Midwestern face, having slept poorly in the motel I'd paid for, managing a stiff adieu resembling the safety catch on Freyling's nine-millimeter. George came over to me and we both tried to pretend that the hug we exchanged signified something more than duty. I wondered if he looked that sour in front of his classes. Could be that a puss of perpetual disapprobation is just what's wanted in nineteenth-century historians. The ones I knew did have a penchant for walking around looking like grandfather clocks, like earnest, scowling busts of Brahms or Garibaldi.

George offered to drop Jill at the station but they really didn't have the room and anyway I wanted to drive her myself in my rented car, didn't want her to leave me just yet. George can't love me but he's stolid and steadier than I ever was. He's so irrevocably grown up I suppose he resents being made to feel a child in my presence. Jill, on the other hand, is like a pack of cards, you never know what'll turn up, which Jill it's going to be this time. The sullen, provocative adolescent who experimented with sex and drugs is still in there, also the Daddy's girl overwhelmed by her tumultuous puberty, and the sentimental idealist who spent a year changing the world and feeding a tapeworm in Guatemala, a year during which Sheila and I never took a deep breath. After she moved back to New York she began her interminable analysis, ran through men by the dozen, and never married a one. But she worked hard, worked her way up as a freelance and now she's on the staff of *Business Monthly*, of all things. She specializes in what she calls "bios." She's got a real flair for interviewing greedy men and potent women. I wonder if it's owing to a concealed identification with their competitiveness and success or the opposite, an antipathy to their relentless, well-nourished egos. But I wouldn't dare ask.

It was a short ride to the train station and Jill, tough interviewer that she is, didn't waste a minute. "Well, Daddy, what're you going to do now?"

"Go on, I suppose. Figure out how to be a widower. See how well I can stand it for a few more years.

"You're not even sixty-six."

"Ha!"

"They'll be all over you, you know."

"Who?"

"Florida widows, of course. You're a live one."

She sounded accusing, as if I had already picked out a wicked stepmother for her, as though the ink were even then drying on the pre-nuptial agreement, the two couches squeezed into one condo.

"I don't feel all that alive," I said candidly. "In fact, I don't feel much like living. I don't know how to go about it on my own."

"So then *don't* do it on your own. Find a new companion, let one find you."

I pulled the car over. "Look, Sweetie. I don't think you've got a very clear idea of what your mother was to me. All that psychoanalysis, all that pulling the family apart, maybe it's led you to underestimate how tangled together your mother and I were, I mean right down to the root."

She put her hand on my arm. "Daddy," she whispered.

"He told you I'm the reason you can't settle on a man, right? Dr. Whatsit, your shrink?"

"Daddy don't—"

But I'd begun to percolate, and it completely slipped my mind that Jill had just lost her mother. "I made fun of you, robbed you of your self-esteem; I was such a megalomaniac that all those little boys couldn't possibly measure up; I left you with unresolved conflicts, repressed traumas, recovered memories of imaginary abuses, ambivalent ambiguities—"

"Stop it."

"You don't get it."

"Stop!"

"It really *is* all my fault. Even if he's an idiot, Whatsit's right! If I'd been with her—"

"Daddy!" she pleaded. Her face was full of tears.

Maybe my daughter was forgiving me, which is what I probably needed just then. There's nothing more disarming than a breakdown and I was having them at regular intervals.

Mother was the one who meted out the punishments, organized the schedules, laid down that baseline of worldly wisdom you never quite shake off, a mixture of prejudices and common sense, attitudes frozen in a past that may even have existed. But like all practical people she lived chiefly in the present and immediate future, a little like the corporate lions and jackals I interview (the men always start by asking if I'm single, the women if I have any kids). Splendid in a crisis, steadfast and loyal to her friends, but having to be propitiated when she lost her temper: chasing George and me around the dining room table, no use threatening us with paternal wrath because we all knew Dad was too much of a child himself and would always identify with our crimes, forgive them in advance, far more at ease teaming up with us to put one over on her, preferring me to George so crudely I couldn't even take pleasure in it but anyway had to pay the price for it with him and Mom, too. And because I didn't marry within acceptable chronological parameters, they didn't know what to make of me and because of Dr. Gutenbach feared for their reputations so now I feel like half an orphan whose father sees her, in so far as he can see her at all, as a complicated sin for which, thanks to his blithely inverted egoism, he believes himself guilty. I ought to write a song about him. Sometimes I Feel Like a Fatherless Child.

When I got back from dropping Jill at the train station, where there had been hugs and semi-sincere resolutions about mutual visits, Paul was waiting for me in the driveway. He rubbed his cheek as if checking to see how much his beard had grown during the morning's perturbations. I had been with Paul often enough to know that rubbing meant Millie-trouble.

I got out of the car and, in my daughter's best manner, asked straight out, "So what's the matter?"

"Well," said Paul, as if with reluctance, "I think you ought to know Millie's been more than a little moody lately, I mean since Sheila died. It's hit her harder than you think, I mean harder than she wants *you* to think."

"Why wouldn't she want me to think that?"

Paul, realizing he'd said more than he should have, just shrugged and looked solemn.

"Come on. Millie could barely stand Sheila. They called each other, what was it? Once a month maybe? Talked for two minutes?"

"I know, I know. But Sheila was Millie's big sister and now's she's the last of the family. It's hit her really hard."

“Ah, the last barrier to mortality gone.”

“What?”

“Never mind. What’re you *actually* trying to tell me, Paul?”

“It’s about the ashes.”

“What about them?”

“Well, you see, Millie wants them. At least *some* of them.”

“What?”

“She told me about it last night. She says she doesn’t trust you to do the right thing, whatever that means.”

“Wait a minute. She wants Sheila’s *ashes*?”

Paul shifted his weight from foot to foot, squirming, rubbing his chin like mad. He moved a little closer, as though afraid Millie would hear him from inside the house. “She’s been talking to them, talking to the ashes. I heard her this morning before you and Jill got up. She was sitting in the kitchen talking to the box.”

He looked so stricken I couldn’t help grinning. “What was she saying?”

Paul didn’t grin back. “I only wanted you to be ready,” he said stiffly, crossing his arms, body lingo for boundary. Sheila often remarked on my annoying knack for finding the wrong things funny.

I started to go in but Paul took my arm. “Are you going to let her have some? That’s what she’s going to ask you.”

I didn’t answer.

Millie was seated at the dining room table which had been cleared of its big funereal flower arrangement and the four silver candlesticks. Before her lay the package of Sheila’s ashes, an open newspaper, a kitchen knife, and six small, ornate boxes, the sort cufflinks and collar studs used to be kept in. Antiques.

"Sit down," she ordered.

I sat.

"I don't expect you to understand this, but I need some of Sheila's ashes."

"Oh?"

She looked at me not beseechingly, not for a moment granting me the right to refuse, but scornfully, as if my feelings didn't enter into the matter at all. I was only being informed.

"I'm going to save some for Jill and George too."

"What?"

"They may want them later on."

"Did they say—"

"They *may*. I'll keep the ashes here. I'll phone them in a week or two and let them know. It's too soon."

I looked down at the box and reminded Millie that Sheila said she wanted her ashes scattered over the bay.

"You already told me. But you didn't do it, did you?"

"I couldn't—"

"Exactly. Then you ought to understand."

"But I'm *going* to. I'm *going* to do it. Just not yet. It's absurd to keep little bits of her here and there. It's, it's sick."

"Oh really? You think it matters that they all go in the drink?"

"I'm not sure any of it matters, Millie."

"Ha! So then you might just as well throw them in the trash, right?"

I was indignant. "If I was going to do that why would I lug them up here?"

Millie grabbed the knife in a way that reminded me of Detective Freyling's story and cut the brown wrapping paper. The box was plain white pine but well made, tongue and groove, nailed shut with brass brads. I watched with horror as Millie inserted the blade to pry open the top. Yet I didn't stop her. As for the coach, he was hiding in the dugout.

You imagine. Ashes. Somebody's ashes. You picture the residue from cigarettes, vestiges of wood fires, a fine dust, an insubstantial powder easily blown away by a strong breeze. Not so. Sheila's ashes were like gravel, mixed with startlingly recognizable bits of bone.

Millie wasn't expecting it any more than I was. "Look!" she cried.

Paul rushed in from the kitchen.

"Jesus, Millie. You scared me."

"Not what you'd expect," I said. Neither of us was prepared actually to *see* Sheila.

Millie poured the ashes out in a mound on the newspaper then used the knife to separate out six thin lines. She worked with the expertise of a cocaine addict, neatly scraping each line into one of her tiny boxes. Paul stood behind her, his hands resting protectively on the back of her chair. I looked up at him and, half-closing his eyes, he shook his head, warning me to let it be. On the phone a few weeks later he told me how Millie had placed each of the boxes at a strategic point in the house, on the landing, in the bathroom, how she was still talking to them. "She says it comforts her to have Sheila around."

Paul re-nailed the pine box, and the next morning I left for Florida with my share of Sheila, with what was left of my wife.

There's the one about the red shoelace and the one about calling the manager a son-of-a-bitch, the one about touching your left testicle and the one about throwing a kiss to some girl in the grandstand. It's a game of superstitions, of rituals—and why? Because between the routine grounders and the strike outs comes the unrepeatable. There are hidden powers all over the diamond. And if there are hidden powers why shouldn't Millie talk to her little boxes, her bits of Sheila? I thought she was going nuts but in fact she's been easier to get along with since the talking began, not as tense, less morose, kind of like she's coming out of a long slump. She doesn't whine so much now. I guess Sheila bears the brunt of her dissatisfaction so, when she wanted to know if it bothers me, I said not at all, dear, not in the least, and didn't even hint that I get spooked sometimes, didn't ask if she'd at least take the box out of the bathroom. My brother-in-law's not a bad guy but Millie never trusted him, insists she didn't want Sheila to marry him in the first place and go off for those two years in Nebraska or Kansas or wherever it was. Sheila was alone in that parking lot she keeps saying. Died by herself, with strangers, in a parking lot. And remember, she says, when he made that stupid joke about her blood pressure, how she shouldn't get so worked up about abortion or HMOs or whatever it was because her face looked like a monkey's bum? She believes he came between them, manipulated Sheila about the nursing home, turned Sheila against her. You can see how it is with his kids, she goes on. George and Allison can't bear him and Jill's still going to that psychiatrist. How could she trust him with all the ashes? Cremation. Sounds like some dairy process. Best to keep my mouth shut.

Ellen Hacker, whom I knew as an optimistic if not altogether merry widow, was the one who nudged me into it. She started in at the pool one afternoon (*Trust me, you need it*) and kept at me (*You'll have a better time than you think*) until I gave in (*Just wait, you'll be grateful*). Though it had a more respectable and less alliterative name, Ellen called it simply Grief Group. It convened on Tuesdays and Fridays in a reception room at the Methodist church. Nobody in particular was in charge. The Group governed itself by the direct democracy of loss. These surprisingly gregarious hens and crones and geezers took me in, waited for me to lose my reserve, prodded me to break down then joshed me to lighten up, asked me out to dinner and movies, popped in to visit, and in general made a fuss over me. Of the three men in the Group, I was by far the youngest and easily the biggest wise-ass. I had at last found my audience; my humor was a hit with the bereft.

Group was not unlike something that might have gone on in high school, the hormonal nonsense included. The one time I asked Ellen to go for a bike ride with me she turned me down with a leer and a wink. "Oh, I'm not at all athletic—except for bedroom sports." Grief may have been the left hand, the intermittent bass, but the busy treble was a sort of continuous salon music. If in Florida nobody has to be old because nobody's young, in Group nobody had to mourn because everybody was bereaved. Loneliness, vacancy, melancholy conveyed no distinction and therefore no special rights. The unwritten rule was that everybody was allowed one and only one crying jag.

They bunched around me; the women teased like Merry Wives badgering Falstaff. Everything went smoothly until that Friday when, in an access of fellow feeling, I told the story of Sheila's ashes. As often happens, what began as a joke wound up a confession.

"Don't tell me you've still got them?" Viola asked indignantly.

"In the bedroom, actually."

General hub-bub, outrage. "Well, I think it's high time you let go," huffed Ellen, who had become a little proprietary about me. "Time you did what Sheila asked you to do."

On this point there was unanimity. The word *closure* was prominently bandied. The next Tuesday Ellen informed me in front of the whole Group that her friend Julie McAllister had promised to take me out on her thirty-footer early the next Saturday. Nothing simpler. Just do it. Of course, I gave in at once, grateful to be bullied.

Julie's about forty-five, a svelte golfer, a good manager of engines, sand traps, watercraft, and me. We hit it off from the moment I came on board with Ellen when she offered me a cup of black coffee and asked with a Bogart twitch if I'd brought the *dingus*.

It was a lovely Saturday. Not much humidity at eight a.m., only a few cirrus filaments stretched above azure water, pelicans sweeping low, gulls wheeling above, real tourist board weather. In just ten minutes Julie's inboard had us off Sheila's favorite beach. A few pallid tourists were already spread out, a gaggle of children splashed in the water. Invisible on the beach road lurked Freyling, leaning photogenically on his bumper, nine-millimeter at his hip, surveying his beat through narrowed Eastwood eyes.

I had hardly slept the night before. I was nervous, the way you get before a final exam. I clutched the pine box with both hands.

"Can we stop here?" I asked.

"Sure," said Julie, cutting the engine.

The boat rocked a little, but I found I was able to stand up without much difficulty. I went to the side and leaned mournfully over it.

"Hey! Aren't you going to *say* something?" Julie asked. "A prayer, a eulogy. *Some*thing."

I set my feet as firmly as I could and looked at the box. Of course I was going to say something, but it was hard to speak in front of the two women, though maybe easier than it would have been had I been alone. Julie came over and patted me manfully on the back. "Hey. Just forget *us* and talk to *her*, to—"

"To Sheila," said Ellen expertly.

Talking to ashes is my sister-in-law's department, I almost said.

I shuffled my way to the stern, turned my back on the women, and held the box out before me like a pagan offering. Bits of language bounced around my head: *ashes to ashes, the curfew tolls the knell of parting day, I heard a fly buzz.*

I took a deep breath and spoke to the box. "I'm sorry, sweetheart, so sorry I wasn't with you in the Winn Dixie parking lot, that I didn't know how to keep you alive, that I haven't even kept you together. I'm sorry for all my tantrums and rotten jokes. I'm sorry things turned out the way they did with the kids. I'm sorry if it's my fault you and Millie weren't closer. I'm sorry for the two awful years in Nebraska. I'm sorry I didn't challenge that cop's racism and for all the times I held my tongue at school and came home and took it out on you. I'm sorry about the Australian pines. I'm sorry this took me so long, old thing. Forgive me. It's awful being without you." My knees were buckling but, as they say, I'd expressed myself.

Then I realized I hadn't opened the box. I couldn't just dump the whole thing in the water. Ashes had to be *scattered.* What a dazzling anti-climax. I turned around, tearful, baffled, chagrined. Julie was there with a screwdriver and an understanding smile. She patted my back again then gently took the box from me and discreetly retreated into the cabin to pry it open. In the meantime, Ellen took my hand, and I realized that I had never heard her speak about her husband.

"Ellen, what was your husband like?"

She smiled almost shyly as she answered, "Actually, my dear, astonishingly like you."

Le Parlement des Amis Imaginaires

It had been a horrible day and, when Faker called me from the airport, I guess I broke down a little. He said his plane was still being fueled so he had at least another half hour and I should tell him everything. Faker Brodsky was a detail man.

"Well, to begin with, I only got a C+ on my geography test, then, in gym, I fell down like a complete spaz, and then at lunch I spilled cranberry-raspberry juice on my yellow skirt which is the worst kind of stain and won't ever come out."

"You know, I find it sometimes will. Try putting a little stain remover on the spot then drip boiling water over it and brush very hard. You could use that hand brush over the kitchen sink."

Faker was the kind of friend who gives advice only when he knows it's likely to work. Most people give advice that has as much chance of working as a chicken of giving milk. They do it just to sound sympathetic and expert. Not Faker. He knew what was irremediable and what wasn't and didn't dwell on the former.

"Where are you off to?" I wanted to know. "Business or pleasure?"

"Dallas—and it's both business *and* pleasure, as it happens."

"Which one's in Dallas, Faker? I really can't keep track."

Faker chuckled. "Fair enough. Sometimes I get mixed up myself. Anyway, in Dallas it's Elaine. I call her the Lady of Shallot. There's a heap of oil equipment I want, too."

Faker Brodsky did better than sailors who have a girl in every port. Because he flew his own plane, he could have a girlfriend—or two—in any place with a landing field. Women liked Faker a lot. He was tremendously rich from the oil business, also highly adventurous, and he looked like a mixture of Harrison Ford, Mark Twain, and John Kennedy, only younger. He had trekked through jungles and deserts. He was as at home in a casino as Bond, James Bond, an advanced skier, a reliable mountain climber, and he had a black belt in judo. Faker owned several houses, but his favorite was the smallest which had the inestimable advantage that I was the only one who knew about it. It was just a log cabin out in the woods although furnished with every conceivable convenience. This was where Faker retreated when he wanted to be alone. When Faker first mentioned his cabin, I told him I understood exactly why he'd want such a special place and that I had mine too. "Oh, I know," he'd said. "In fact, you have three places: let's see, there's the swing in the backyard, sometimes the shed, and then the window seat." About me Faker was never wrong, but sometimes he said his cabin was in Maine and at other times Montana. It wasn't like Faker to make mistakes so I decided he must have two cabins.

"Come on, Julie," Faker insisted. "What was the very *worst* thing that happened today. You can tell *me*."

"I'm not sure I should."

"But it's *me*, it's your pal *Faker*. Come on. Plane and Elaine are waiting."

"Well," I mumbled hesitantly. "I don't want to hurt your feelings."

"Hurt my feelings? Julie, you've never hurt me. I mean, you *can't*."

"All right, then. In the bus, on the way home?"

"Yes, in the bus?" Faker was impatient in the way people are when they're struggling to be patient.

"Molly Stern was sitting next to me?" It was because I was reluctant that I started ending every sentence with a rising voice. Faker had pointed this bad habit out to me before.

"Oh," he said, "Molly Stern. She's—what?—a year older than you?"

"A year and three-quarters. She's in sixth grade."

"And stuck up, as I recall? A little superior, maybe a wee bit arrogant?"

I don't know why, but I suddenly wanted to defend Molly. "She can be nice too."

"Sure," Faker agreed in order to move things along. "So, what happened on the bus with Molly?"

"I just *happened* to mention—I mean it just slipped *out*, you know?"

"Mentioned. . ?" Faker prompted, Dallas and the Lady of Shallot beckoning iridescently below the setting sun.

"I mentioned, well, you."

"Me? Oh, Julie. You know—"

"Yes, yes, I *know*. I'm not *supposed* to. But like I said, it sort of just slipped out." I had dropped the rising voice. Now I was just whining defensively.

"You mean *I* slipped out," he corrected. "So, what did old Molly say?"

"'Who's this Faker Brodsky?' So, I told her, sort of."

"Oh, no. *What* did you tell her exactly?" As I said, Faker was a detail man. All tycoons are.

"Well, I told her how very nice you are and about your plane and the girlfriends and your trip to the rain forest in Brazil when you tamed that monkey."

"You didn't mention the *cabin*, did you?"

"Of course not!"

"Well, that's a relief. Okay, so what did Molly say *then*?"

"She didn't actually say anything about *you*. It's what she said about *me*."

"I can imagine." Faker was alert and perspicacious, qualities certain women appreciated as much as his money, good looks, and houses.

"Molly made fun of me, and she told the other kids, and they all suck up to Molly, so *they* made fun of me too. Oh, and it started raining this afternoon. It's just *pouring* out now. And Dad called and said he'd be late."

"Well," Faker observed, "you *have* had a bad day. But it could have been worse, you know, and it still might get better." Dear, encouraging Faker.

"Oh. Dad's home. I can hear the car door."

"Great. Then I'm off to Dallas. The Big D and the bewitching E."

"Okay."

"I'll call you tonight."

"Please do."

"Okay, sure. One last thing, Julie. Can you just forget about what Molly said? Will you promise to do that for me?"

"I promise to *try*. I'll do my best."

"All I can ask. And remember, sweetie, any landing's a good landing," he added breezily then clicked off.

There were occasions when I might have been afraid of my father, but I never was. When he seemed mad at me, I knew that he wasn't, not really. It was his earnestness that undermined him, an anxiety not to be perfect but just to be adequate. He put me first and yet he couldn't *always* put me first. There was his job and the job paid for both of us and I knew this and yet whenever his work kept him from me—when it made him late, for instance, or when he had to leave me with a cold or a stomach ache, or when he had to work after I went to bed and I wouldn't go to bed—well, naturally, the frustration had to come out *some*how. When he was really angry it was always with himself. All this I only sensed vaguely; it was Faker who explained it to me. He advised me to tell Dad I understood it all perfectly well and didn't mind a bit. So, Dad and I talked about it and Faker was right. That talk made things easier, though Dad often seemed to me like a clenched fist. Faker had spelled it out. "It's love versus duty, Julie, one of the great tragic themes. It's the human condition. Built-in."

So, Dad got home late that night. He was only a half-an-hour late, nothing to me, but I reminded myself he had been pumping up his blood pressure for all those thirty minutes. I ran to the door and tried to spread oil over his troubled waters.

"Welcome home, Dad!" I threw my arms around him, mindful to convey joy and not resentment, not relief.

"Oh, sweetheart, I'm *so* sorry," he lamented, dumping his briefcase and tearing at his tie. "It was terrible. I got held up, phone call after phone call, and then the traffic—slow idiots, dumb idiots, and slow dumb idiots."

I wanted to tell him about my awful day and knew that I would, later on, but now I beamed at his complaints, aware that they were really excuses. I remembered what he'd said when I was sick, and he held my head over the toilet, and told me to let it all out. I let him get it all out.

While Dad was making dinner, I fired up the computer. Instead of playing games, I did a little desultory surfing. I checked the capital of Kentucky (stupid Frankfort); I looked up Janis Joplin (Dad liked her), then I typed in the phrase Molly had used. A web site on parenting came up with a devastatingly smug, authoritative declaration from Doctor T. M. Brough:

> Imaginary friends are common and seldom a problem, so long as they don't prevent your child from carrying on a normal life. It's generally not a good idea to talk your child out of them; better to ask what the friend says and does. You can use the friend as a window into your child. Imaginary friends reveal creativity and are not necessarily signs of stress or loneliness. Whether or not you encourage them, imaginary friends will usually disappear within six months.

My father and I didn't eat together. He liked listening to the news on the radio and I enjoyed watching old sit-coms. We also had entirely different diets and ate at different speeds. To this day, whenever I hear the theme for *All Things Considered* I hear the sizzle of meat. I was a half-hearted vegetarian, a carbohydrate queen, as Dad put it. But I liked most vegetables, except for lima beans and broccoli, and I loved his red sauce, of which he made a pot every Saturday. I may have been slim—"imperially slim," Dad said—but I didn't starve, which I suspect he was afraid I would. At first, we did try eating together, the way we all used to do, at the table, and with cloth napkins too. But it was really tense. The night he promulgated the new policy, Dad confessed to me how much he'd always detested his own family dinner table, everybody watching and criticizing, quizzing and probing. He was exhilarated, as if he'd just invented a new machine or found the perfect recipe for fudge. So, we began to eat separately.

The enchanted time, our together time, the time when my father and I belonged exclusively to one another, came after dinner and lasted about an hour and a half, bath included. When I say exclusive, I mean it. Neither of us would take phone calls or plead homework or—in one memorable case of oblivious rudeness—waste a moment of the time on the couple we'd invited to supper. Poor Dad. It was one of his bosses too, and the man barely spoke to him for two weeks and all my father had to offer when finally confronted with his unspeakable discourtesy was the lame truth, that it simply hadn't occurred to him that *they* didn't know about the sacred hour and a half. That's how hard he tried.

What did we do in those ninety minutes? There was quite a range. Lots of games, of course, Boggle and Parcheesi to Spite and Malice, and there were home-made ones as well. One of our favorites was Role Reversal. I would be the strict but understanding parent and he'd be the incorrigible but contrite little boy. The best was Treasure Hunt. While I was in the bath, keeping up the chatter, giving the blow-by-blow of my entire day, Dad would hide ten items around the house—socks, staplers, can openers, sneakers. He'd make a list and, once I was clean, dry, and pajamaed, I'd get ten minutes to find them all. We also made use of a portable tape recorder, singing mock-fugues or calling imaginary baseball games and horse races. Sometimes, if we'd both had hard days, we'd just tumble on the floor and watch whatever the networks were dishing out.

After the games, the hunts, the TV, I'd get into bed and be read to. It surprises me now how quickly all this became routine. My father must have thought it all out, the rigid yet open scheduling of a clenched fist.

On that particular night, the night after Molly humiliated me on the bus, the night of Faker's flight to Dallas, my father proposed a game of Treasure Hunt. But we never got around to it. I let it all out while I was in the bath, let it out even more than I had with Faker that afternoon.

In fact, after the bad test, the mortification in gym, the stained skirt, and Molly Stern, I complained about Faker too, that traitor, jetting off to yet another of his scores of lady friends and more wheeling-dealing while handing me anodynes, telling me to just forget what Molly'd said.

Dad listened, commiserated, made excuses for Faker, blamed himself for not going over those state capitals with me one more time. He even said he'd give the stain remover and boiling water a shot on the yellow skirt. But I was no less blue.

"Anything *else*?" he asked tentatively, the way I imagine one might ask a bomb if it's ticking.

I told him about know-it-all Dr. T. M. Brough. "If he's right, then Faker's going to disappear *next* month," I whimpered and completely lost it.

Dad looked as if he took me seriously. I think fathers have to master the furrowed brow, the stroked chin and keep up their high seriousness in the face of any absurdity, so long as their child feels it deeply enough.

I got out of the bath, and he enfolded me in the big soft towel. He rubbed my shoulders and my head and my bum. I can't remember that he said anything though, not until I got into bed.

Dad tucked me in carelessly. I could see his mind was someplace else but had no clue where. He wasn't looking at me but at the window.

"Julie?" he began gently.

"Yes?"

"You remember my telling you how your mother and I met?"

"You know I love that story. You met at college when there was this mix-up, and she thought you were somebody else, and you let her go on thinking it for a whole hour before you told her. You said you needed that hour."

Dad smiled because I remembered or because he was remembering too. He sat down on the bed and rubbed my quilt a little.

"Yes, but I never told you *why* we met, how that wonderful mix-up came about."

I was a little shocked. It's disquieting to hear corrections to a creation myth. "*Why* you met? You mean it *wasn't* a mix-up?"

"The accident wasn't *entirely* an accident, Julie, which, by the way, means *you* weren't an accident."

"Never thought I was," I groused. This was altogether too serious a conversation; Dad was sounding almost grave.

"Most children *are* accidents, I'm afraid," he said.

This was getting off the point. I wasn't much interested in how I figured in their story, let alone statistics on unwanted pregnancies. I wanted to hear more about that famous confusion of identities, when, as Dad had put it, a blind date turned into *the* blind date, when the *wrong* miraculously became the *right*.

He smiled and moved a little nearer. "It's a big secret," he said, "a secret your mother and I shared. I wasn't sure when or even *whether* to tell you about it, but now I think the time's come. I mean tonight. I mean right now. Ready?"

Were they spies or something? This was more exciting than *The Wind in the Willows*. I waited for Dad to go on. He was speaking in an unusually low voice, not as if somebody else might be listening but because what he was saying was this "big secret," the *real* story of how my parents met, secret of secrets.

"Only your mother and I knew about it, but Faker Brodsky may know too. I'm not sure; you'll have to ask him. He hasn't by any chance mentioned anything about me and your mom, has he?"

I shook my head. "Not about how you met."

"All right, then. Here's how it happened."

I looked at him suspiciously, uncertain if he was mocking me, if this was just Molly and the insufferable doctor with a wistful smile, humoring me.

"Your Dr. Brough is right, so far as he goes. What he doesn't know is that forty years ago the friends he calls imaginary came to the same conclusion. An average of six months of joyous life, of delightful companionship, and then extinction. Poof! Non-existence. Generations had vanished as suddenly as that. You can imagine the urgency of the first ones to figure it out, what a crisis it was for them, how they needed to spread the news. And this is how *Le Parlement des Amis Imaginaires* came to be held."

"The what?"

"In those days, French was still the language of global diplomacy, so the organizers gave their assembly a French name. In English it would be the Parliament of Imaginary Friends."

Though lying in my own bed, I felt myself teetering, uncertain whether to challenge or play along, to laugh or believe. I decided it was best just to keep my mouth shut. I would be taking all this up with Faker later, when he phoned from Dallas.

"The assembly convened in Greece, in one of those old, abandoned theaters. The place was crammed with delegates from all over the earth. The sharpest, the one who had figured things out, laid the problem before the crowd and invited suggestions. A solution, all agreed, was vital. And they needed it at once.

"An intelligent, rather forward imaginary friend from Japan named Miranda Matsumoto stood up and offered her analysis. 'As I see it,' Miranda said, 'the problem is that the children to whom we devote ourselves, including my own darling Tomiko, *outgrow* us, as the adults put it. But it's the adults themselves who are behind this. Oh, they think of us as charming at first but soon they become fearful and disapproving. Then there are the older children, not only the ones without imagination but also the ones that are proud they've *outgrown* us—they put on the pressure too. Our existence is *that* fragile. The question is, what is to be done?'

"Here Robbie Belfry, from Scotland, made a reasonable suggestion. He said the issue was obviously to preserve the children's belief and this belief, as Ms. Matsumoto had just shown, was under attack at its weakest point, from elders and peers and even *doctors*. Robbie's suggestion was that they all do their utmost to convince their children to lie. . . to tell the others they no longer believed but to go on doing so in secret."

Here I couldn't help interjecting, "To *lie*?"

"That's right. To pretend and mislead and keep it all to themselves. Well, you can imagine the uproar in the amphitheater. Some supported Robbie's idea and others thought it outrageous and impractical while still others simply refused to tell their children to lie to their parents. Finally, an extremely smart fellow named Hilarius Ludovicus Bumbalius, from Finland, took the floor.

"'The issue before us isn't the children's belief but our existence. What's needed,' he said, 'isn't thousands of believers. We're unlikely to get them and, besides, it would scatter our efforts when what we need is to concentrate them. No, what we require is *one* believer, one for all of us. As long as this one keeps it up for us all, as long as he or she manages to go *on* believing, no—poof!'

"'But he, or she, would have to be extraordinary,' somebody cried out. 'Think of the burden!' 'We'd need a saint!' 'What a terrible responsibility!' 'It's too much to expect.' 'And if they disclosed the secret it would be curtains for him or her—not to mention for us!'

"'You're all right,' said Hilarius. 'We'll have to help him or her, offer solace and comfort and companionship but never intrude, never mob them. We'll send a delegate, especially in the worst hours.'

"'But he or she is going to grow up,' somebody pointed out.

"'Then he'll have new needs for us to satisfy, that's all,' Hilarius said, unwilling to give up his idea.

"At this point Miranda took the floor again. 'As for me, I like Hilarius's proposal but would like to offer a small amendment. I think *two* would be better than one. After all, what if the child we choose should die suddenly or just change her mind? We'd be gone before we knew it. Poof!"

"Well, after that there was a lot of discussion. Gertrude Mombasa, from Nigeria, was quite upset. She asked. 'We'd still be able to stay with our *own* children now, wouldn't we? I mean until they *outgrow* us?' 'Why not?' said Hilarius. 'Of course,' seconded Miranda, 'for as long as possible.'

"And so, it was decided to pick *two* children. Encouraged by the success of her amendment, Miranda then proposed that one should be a boy and the other a girl and, in a moment of inspiration, that it should be arranged that they fall in love and get married. 'That way,' she said shrewdly, 'they could share the secret and support each other.'"

I yawned and looked my father right in the eye. "You and mom?"

He nodded. "And now—you, sweetheart."

I yawned again. "And now me."

"Now, go to sleep," said my father in a whisper.

Faker phoned in the middle of the night. I began to tell him about *Le Parlement des Amis Imaginaires,* but he said he already knew all about it. They *all* did. He was ecstatic. He positively crooned. "Oh, Julie. This is exactly what I've been hoping for. But look, I'm with Elaine at the moment. Let's talk about it more tomorrow. I'll call from the plane. I've got to go to Cleveland, of all places."

"Cleveland?"

"Look, are you all right, Julie?"

"Yeah. I'm fine."

"Sure?"

"Yep."

"Not *lonesome* or anything?"

"Nope, just sleepy."

"Forget about Molly yet?"

"Nearly."

"Good. In that case, sleep tight."

Petite Suite Non Résolue

1. Drame Amoureux de la Salle D'Audience. *Sarabande en ut-mineur pour piano et hautbois silencieux - frustrant, plein de suspense, épuisant, fastidieuse, et goûtant comme une dacquoise rance*

On May 15 of last year, at four in the afternoon, Officers Desiderio, a veteran, and Verlock who had only a year on the job, responded to a call from a woman reporting her son's erratic behavior. "She said her son is twenty-three and mentally challenged," reported the dispatcher. "And unarmed. I asked."

When the officers arrived, they found a man on the lawn walking rapidly back and forth, alternately mumbling to himself and yelling at a woman near the open front door who was wringing her hands. These were Ryan McKenna and his mother Vera.

Desiderio told his partner to stay by their vehicle and approached McKenna with his hands up and speaking soothingly. McKenna lunged suddenly at Desiderio and wrenched his pistol from its holster which the officer had routinely unfastened on exiting the patrol car. Hollering and swearing, McKenna, who weighed over two hundred pounds, knocked Desiderio to the ground and shot him point-blank four times before Verlock tackled him, twisted the gun from McKenna's hand, kneeled on his back, and cuffed him while screaming at the woman to call 911.

Jack Desiderio was well known in town, the father of three children. His wife was secretary of the PTA. The town wanted justice but was going to have to wait for it. Ryan McKenna had a long history of emotional issues. His father took off when the boy was seven and his problems became obvious. The boy's care was down to his mother and what help she could extract from the public schools and the state.

The district attorney had McKenna examined for competency. The state psychiatrist said that, while certainly not normal in all respects, the man was sufficiently fit to be charged and stand trial.

Vera McKenna, who was barely eating or sleeping, contacted the social worker who saw her son once a month. The social worker advised her to get an outside opinion and even found a psychiatrist who would work *pro bono*. Her opinion was that Ryan had a psychotic episode and, under pressure from the public and the police union, the D.A. was out to convict Ryan of murder in the first degree.

"It's yours," said the managing editor to Victor Bramosa, a reward for having done "a passable job," as the editor put it, covering local sports, then a celebrity divorce, followed by a tangled bribery case in the Assessor's office.

The courtroom was almost as hard to get into as a Springsteen concert. But Victor's press credentials and setting his alarm for six a.m. scored him a great seat—first row behind the prosecutor's table with a prime view of the defense's. Mrs. McKenna sat at the other end of the row. An elderly lady held her hand.

Victor had arrived before the lawyers and their assistants. The D.A., who was prosecuting himself, had four assistants. The public defender, an old liberal crusader inured to the public's hatred, had just one.

Miranda Vocelli was two years out of law school. She was dressed professionally in a black pantsuit and white blouse. Her long straight hair was black too. Victor couldn't take his eyes off her, this woman with dark eyes and a figure the pantsuit couldn't entirely hide. Her seriousness added to her attraction. *Love comes in at the eye*, Victor's favorite poet wrote. *Coup de foudre* say the French, which is better than love at first sight, though it means the same thing. It certainly did for Victor Bramosa.

The trial lasted two weeks for the first of which Victor stared in delighted agony at Miranda Vocelli. His reporting suffered. "This is the best you can do?" scolded his editor. "Christ, the fluffy blonde on TV interviewed Desiderio's widow—tears and everything. Get on the stick."

On Thursday of the first week, at the end of the day's proceedings, Victor worked up the nerve to approach Miranda Vocelli. He said he was a reporter and asked for an interview. She scoffed and said she had to run. By then he'd found out where she went to school, that she played varsity volleyball, where she was born, and that she wasn't married. There could be a boyfriend, but she didn't do social media and who could he ask except her?

The next day, he asked her to have dinner with him.

"Too busy," she said brusquely. It wasn't a downright refusal.

He tried again on Monday.

"The crisis is coming," she said. "Battle of the experts. We're meeting tonight."

The next morning, the state put their shrink on the stand. That took the whole day, mostly consumed by cross-examination. Miranda wrote notes furiously and handed them to her boss.

"Too exhausted," she said when, at the end of the day, he suggested a drink.

The defense's psychiatrist took the stand the next day. The public defender had her go through McKenna's medical record in detail and explain her diagnosis of a psychotic break which took the form of paranoia. She was very cool, not fazed by the D.A.'s cross-examination, not even by ruthless mockery which the jury appeared to enjoy.

"What about this weekend? Dinner? Lunch? Coffee? Hiking? Shopping? You name it."

Miranda shook her head. "Maybe when we get a verdict."

As soon as he was alone, Victor gave himself a fist bump.

Closing arguments were on Thursday morning. The jury began deliberations after lunch.

On Friday morning, everybody gathered, but there was no verdict.

Between Friday night and Saturday afternoon, Victor wrote his best and longest article on the trial. He focused on the vital issue, the respective merits of the prosecutor's contention that McKenna was legally sane and criminally responsible and the defense's rebuttal that he was neither. Because of Miranda, the article was slanted toward the defense. He just made his deadline, so it was published on Sunday.

The managing editor let him have it. "I've had about thirty calls and more emails than when that moron Rowley got the governor's husband's name wrong. You haven't noticed the mood of your fellow citizens, aka our subscribers? You want this ship to go belly up?"

No one was more eager for a verdict—any verdict—than Victor Bramosa, aching for Miranda when he was conscious, dreaming about her when he wasn't.

Everybody convened again on Monday but were sent away, verdictless. Miranda's reply when Victor asked her to lunch was delivered with annoyance. "I told you, when the case is over. *Maybe*."

Deliberations went on for another day. On Thursday, the jury came in looking tight-lipped and stone-faced.

"You're unable to reach a verdict?" the judge asked the jury foreman who turned red and said, "Yes—that is, no."

The D.A. was furious. Miranda hugged the public defender. Ryan didn't move. His mother fainted. The crowd groaned in protest. Mrs. Desiderio, who had brought her children, wailed.

Mistrial. Hung jury. Retrial. The case wasn't over.

Victor Bramosa looked longingly at Miranda Vocelli, who didn't look back.

2. La Femme dans Mon Lit. *Adagio en Si-Mineur pour Violoncelle Seul - perplexe, échoué, pas assez brûlant d'envie mais en fait, avec un sentiment refoulé comme un rot*

A last-minute crisis kept me at work until nearly six o'clock, the hour when I'm accustomed to eating dinner. Before leaving the office, I phoned my local Thai place and ordered Pad See Ew to pick up on the way home. An accident backed traffic up, and by the time I got to the restaurant the noodles were cold. It was that kind of day. Pulling into the driveway felt good; it always does.

During her brief widowhood—before she retired, remarried, moved to Florida, and died—my mother used to complain of having to come home to *a dark cold empty house*. At the time, I was sharing a two-bedroom with slovenly George and punk-rock-besotted Judd. *A dark cold empty house* sounded ideal to me; it still does. I was raised in a duplex, spent four years in dormitories, then the shared apartment with G and J. I saved up and, when I told my roommates I was going to move out and buy a place of my own, they were sure I'd get a condo in town, "close to work," said George, "near the bars and clubs," said Judd. What I craved, though, was a place with nobody on the other side of any wall.

I found a just-affordable suburban Cape with a driveway, a magnolia, a maple, and a hedged-in yard. I planted hosta, myrtle, and two lignum vitae trees because the garden-store expert said they were fast-growing. The place fitted me like a shortstop's old glove, or a badger's burrow.

When I got home, I was so famished that I didn't even bother changing into jeans. I switched on the radio, took in the latest bad news while microwaving the noodles, and wolfed it down with a glass of iced tea. Then I went into the living room, flopped on the couch, and switched on the TV. I almost dropped off halfway through an *NCIS* before anybody fired a gun or blew anything up. I decided to make it an early night and plodded groggily upstairs.

A woman was curled in my bed with the duvet pulled up, one naked arm exposed. She looked a little like an actress I'd seen in an episode of *Midsomer Murders,* one of the victims. Her body had been discovered similarly curled up in the back seat of a Land Rover parked in front of a thatched cottage.

I was on the point of checking for a pulse when I saw that she was taking soft, even breaths. Relieved, I stepped back from the bed. The woman's mouth was slightly open, showing white teeth and a sliver of pink tongue. She was lying near the edge of the bed, almost as if leaving space for me. She turned, raised a shoulder, drew up her knees, and sighed like somebody who needed a back rub and was getting it.

What to do? Should I wake her? I decided against it. I yawned.

My little house has a small second bedroom with a cheap twin mattress on the floor. It had only been used once, when my nephew broke up a trip to New York by spending the night.

I took sheets and pillowcases from the linen closet as quietly as I could.

In the office, phones are always ringing or playing ring tones; there are informal greetings, bad jokes, sports talk, pinging emails, arguments, whispered gossip. I liked the silence of my snug home. In the small bedroom, the quiet felt denser, as if it had been compressed. I tiptoed into the bathroom, took off my clothes, put on my pajamas, brushed my teeth as soundlessly as I could, went back to the little bedroom, closed the door, made up the bed, and tried not to think about the woman in my bed. I was nodding. I needed to sleep and wondered if she would be gone in the morning.

I lay on my back and shut my eyes, but the drowsiness evaporated. The house was quiet, but the silence felt precarious. Despite myself, I listened hard. I hadn't seen any discarded clothing on the floor of my bedroom. The woman in my bed must be clothed.

I rolled on to my side and reviewed my relationships with women. All but the last had ended quickly, by mutual consent and without drama. The last was different. It had gone on for nearly two years and ended badly, which perhaps was why it was the last. I had broken it off without meaning to, without premeditation, seemingly on impulse. The words just escaped me before I could call them back. She was married; I had no idea how happily because she never mentioned her husband's name and I understood I wasn't to ask. Sometimes I thought her silence was meant to spare me, at others that she was roping me off from her real life. I sometimes felt that I only existed for her during the hours we were together, in those golden, stolen afternoons, while I thought of her all the time. Did she love her husband? Me? Both of us or neither? To ask would have been a risk, a violation of a tacit contract. We could talk about politics, books, work, movies, our childhoods, history, theology, technology, the national debt, but never the essential thing. The secret relationship made the two of us a secret. Our bond was intimate but inconsequential. The arrangement worked until the moment it didn't, the moment I opened my mouth and blew it to smithereens. I believed I had acted on a sudden spurt of resentment for coming last on her list of priorities; but that night I considered things differently. I had felt humiliated because my side of the emotional scale outweighed hers. Anyway, it happened all at once. She had phoned to cancel our tryst, not for the first time. But I had asked why. Wasn't she free? Her answer was two full seconds of silence, two decisive seconds. The hiatus might have meant a lot of things, but to me it signified only one. "Nothing," I found myself saying, "Nothing is better than this." It burst from me like a cough or a sneeze. *Nothing is better than this*. These were the very words I had whispered into her ear the first time we'd gone to bed together. Nothing is better than *this* had flipped irrevocably to *Nothing* is better than this.

Happiness makes us vulnerable, love more so. I took that nothing to heart and killed off the instinct for something, for intimacy. I chose the harmless, reliable pleasures of books, music, movies, work, gardening, hiking alone, biking alone. I puttered proprietarily around the house, pleased as ever to know that nobody was on the other side of its walls.

I got up, went to look. The woman in my bed was dreaming. I could see her eyes moving under their lids. What could she be dreaming of? Surely not of being where she was. She must have gotten into the house while I was at work, Goldilocks sneaking into the bears' snug den. I must have left a door unlocked, a window unlatched. It seemed imperative not to wake her. I noticed her left ear beneath a swirl of dark hair. It was a small, perfectly formed ear, like a child's. Her cheek was as smooth as a child's too. In fact, looking down on her in the moonlight coming through the window, I felt like a father checking on his little girl, assuring himself that she was safe, sleeping comfortably, prepared to do mortal battle with anyone who might threaten her.

I looked again for clothing, searching into the corners and the closet. But there were no clothes, no shoes either. Could she have put her things away in my dresser? It seemed improbable. If she'd arrived naked, had she been stripped, fleeing from an attacker? Had she escaped and run to my house, tried the door, and found it unlocked? But I was always careful about the locks.

I went down to the kitchen and turned on the light. How had she gotten in? I checked to see if the back door had been forced or a window broken. The house was tight as a safe-deposit box, or a coffin. Of course, it was possible that for once I had left a door or window open, that she had made her way in and then locked up behind her. If she had been running from an attacker, she would have done that. But it seemed unlikely.

I tiptoed back up to my bedroom. She had moved. Now she was stretched out on her right side, two pillows under her head, the duvet pushed down. Her left shoulder and one breast were exposed, and I shyly pulled the duvet back over her. Stepping quietly to the closet, I opened the door slowly, took my bathrobe from its hook, and laid it on the floor beside the bed. Then I returned to my exile in the small room with the little mattress.

I finally fell into a fitful sleep but that ended when the sun came up. There were no curtains in the spare bedroom. I was briefly disoriented, surprised to find myself where I was. My watch was still on my wrist, and I saw that it was only a few minutes after six, forty-five minutes before I usually got up to go to work. My clock-radio was in the other room, but I hadn't set the alarm.

I put on my clothes from the day before and tried to think of what to say to the woman when she woke. The phrase "home invasion" came into my head trailing images of thugs in black balaclavas wielding kitchen knives, interlopers destroying the inviolability of my haven. I almost chuckled. In the next room was a naked, helpless, vulnerable woman. She was at my mercy.

I imagined a domestic scene in the kitchen. I would make coffee. The aroma would wake her, and she would come downstairs in my robe. Would she like a bagel with raisin bran or prefer eggs and toast with strawberry jam? Tea rather than coffee?

I checked my watch again. I had to be on the road before seven-thirty. I suddenly thought of an idea I could add, then some better-turned phrases. It was an important report, the fruit of a month's work, the only item on the agenda of the big Friday meeting.

Nature called. I went to the downstairs bathroom. It was nearly seven o'clock. Time to act. I went back upstairs, not on tiptoes this time.

The bedroom curtains were pulled back. Sunlight streamed in. My robe was gone. The bed was empty. The two pillows were fluffed and set neatly side by side. The duvet was pulled tight.

I rushed back downstairs, dashed through the living room and into the kitchen. It was empty too but there was a piece of paper in the middle of the table, torn from the pad I keep by the phone. In a rounded feminine hand was a short message. "Better this way. I'll put the robe in the mail."

3. Sur un Pont. *Duo en si bémol-mineur pour violon et alto - hésitant, révélateur, avec beaucoup des rimes et approchant presque la sympathie sinon la compréhension*

Disappointed, directionless, Fernlicht walked out of the theater along with a couple dozen couples and a few single people like himself. Not wanting to go home, he found himself making for the river that divided the city. Like most commuters, he had crossed the bridge countless times but never before on foot.

Traffic was light and, of course, indifferent to a single pedestrian who might be homeless, suicidal or—worse—homicidal. He strode slowly down the narrow sidewalk to the middle of the bridge where he paused and leaned against the cement balustrade. The two parts of the city shuddered. To Fernlicht, they looked like huge, anxious armies drawn up on either side of a dark no-man's-land, streetlights like so many campfires. Far down the river he could see the foundries sparking, power plants seething. Even at this hour, he thought, admiring the way low clouds blushed red like an early evening sky from an aquarelle by Turner.

The bridge had been a great civic enterprise. Engineers with mustaches and eyeshades had pored over plans. Granite, quarried from northern mountains, had been rolled south in huge wagons, draft horses straining, teamsters shouting. Battalions of immigrants had driven the piles, carried hods, risked their lives in the caissons, laid bricks, twisted cables, raised them. Last had come the sculptors who wore smocks and had wild hair, unconventional yet respected men. Politicians from wards on both sides of the river claimed to be wise and far-seeing for raising the taxes for the project. As it took shape, idle citizens gathered on both banks to watch the work. They asked each other or whom the bridge was going to be named; they talked about how their lives would be eased when the span was finished. Schoolchildren were taken on field trips by teachers who pointed to the arches so they would understand how Rome had endured its eight centuries.

On the morning of the grand opening, there had been a splendid ceremony. Thousands of people from both sides of the river turned out. The bridge itself was as gaily festooned as a new battleship. Picnics were spread on what were then still grassy banks. Three bands played, two choruses sang, and young people lined up behind painted barriers at either end, eager to join the *avant-garde,* the first to cross, something to tell their grandchildren. The governor made a fitting speech and then his brilliantly dressed lady cut a ribbon. The mayor smiled and shook every extended hand. As the last barriers came down, cheers filled the sky like factory smoke.

Fernlicht lingered in the middle of the bridge. Graffiti in serpentine scrawls marred the cement. A water nymph had lost her nose and half an arm. He could hear the water flowing inkily beneath him, innocent yet insidious. If you stared down at it long enough, the river began to appear more substantial than the bridge which began to feel almost imaginary.

Another walker came toward Fernlicht strolling slowly, unhurried. An open peacoat flapped around his torso, which was a substantial one. The orange tip of his cigarette brightened once then arced toward the river, trailing sparks. The man passed behind Fernlicht, took a few more steps, then stopped and leaned over the balustrade.

"Good evening," said Fernlicht.

"Good enough, I guess. Not raining anyway." The man had a flat voice. Fernlicht couldn't read anything into it.

"Hm," he said.

"Ask you something?"

"Sure."

"It's pretty easy, isn't it?"

"What?"

"Being white."

"Well," Fernlicht answered, "the white part's easy but the *being* can get tricky."

The man laughed. "Spoken like a white guy, kind's been to college."

"Right you are. To college and then some. In fact, I used to teach in a college. So, there you are."

The man in the peacoat sighed then broke into a kind of sing-song recitation. Fernlicht marveled at the rhymes.

"*I sucked the bottle and I worked the docks; I dug Aristotle and I busted rocks; I been to college and I been to jail; I grabbed some knowledge but I jumped bail. . . .* So, what'd you teach?"

"Hard to say if I taught anything. Teaching being a transitive verb, you'd have to ask my students about that. But the subject was history. I'm sure I didn't teach history anything."

"The foul and shameful cavalcade of the centuries. The procession of folly over a river full of tears. Shit, man. *His*tory."

"That's about sums it up, all right. Just one damned thing after another, like the fella said."

The man broke into rhyme a second time. "*Herodotus, Thucydides, old Tacitus, Maimonides, fat Suetonius, mostly erroneous, long tall Gibbon tied up with ribbon, and Jules Michelet, that grand*

Français, so all you know's as white as snow, and all's I know is old Jim Crow."

"Excuse me. Are you making these up on the spot?"

"Yes and no," the man said indifferently. "Why should you care?"

"I was only asking."

"Look, white folks'll listen to the music, and that's it. *Listen*, not dig, you *dig*? Music's abstract so you can pretty well ignore what it's saying, can't you? If you want. You can sentimentalize, sympathize, idolize, and never *realize*. Now street rap's different. Different even from walking blues. It's *all* words, man. Ruthless stuff, like these kids kill you for a quarter, off each other for a pair of high-tops with the right name on 'em. You say you want to know if I extemporize? Jingles everywhere, man."

"Words, words, words."

"Yeah, that's it. When the old fool asks what you reading, my lord. Hamlet raps real good." The man gave a snort, turned away, cupped his hands, lit another cigarette. "Wife and I had a disagreement. What're *you* doing here?"

"I went to a movie. It depressed me. I felt choked, needed air, took a walk and found myself out here. On the bridge."

"What was the movie about?"

"Nothing. Explosions. That's what depressed me."

"Know what you mean. Wet goods for babies."

"So, it's hard? I mean being black?"

"Shit. Being *black*? Just the opposite of your little wisecrack. The being's easier than the black. We're famous for *being*, right? Being durable. Being long-suffering. Being humane. Being angry.

Being oversexed, drug-crazed, dangerous, forgiving, and *magical.* One big pain in the ass is what *being black* is. Still, you got to be proud of being history's incubi." He laughed. "*Solitude, soul food, acting rude, talking crude, real bad dude. . . Negritude.*"

"So, what did you and your wife disagree about?"

"You gotta ask you ain't been married."

"I used to be married."

"Well then."

"Yeah."

"So, we live with it. Never sure why. You got to be white, I got to be black. It's my black makes you white."

"Hm," Fernlicht said thoughtfully.

"But what's *with* you, man? Going to movies by yourself, walking around the city after dark. Out on this bridge. *Used* to be married, *used* to teach college. No offense man, but it's like you dead."

"No, not dead. A little thirsty though. What do you say to a beer?"

"I say thanks but I'm going home."

"Now?"

"Yeah. Now. Home."

"Well, okay. Good night, then."

"Good enough."

"At least it's not raining."

Already vanishing into the shadows of the great cables, the man turned once and chuckled. "Yeah. Good *enough.*" Then he started back the way he'd come, rapping to himself. "*I'm goin' dig the spill of Sugar Hill. Now that's fine precipitation, incantation, insemination with representation.* The best, man."

After that, Fernlicht also left the bridge, walking irresolutely in the opposite direction.

Petite Suite de Musées

1. *Musée Minimale - scherzo en ré majeur pour piano et violon, assez joli, assez sérieux, déroutant, minuscule, et modestement informatif*

The Musée Pietro Francese occupies a second-floor room in a small building on the Via Milite Ignotus in the town of Ventimiglia.

The nationality of Pietro Francese (? – 1532) is ambiguous. The surname is Italian for French, but in France he is referred to as Pierre de Varenna, after a town on the shore of Lake Como. This suggests that the French saw him as Italian, and the Italians thought him a Frenchman. It is fitting, then, that the museum bearing his name should be in an Italian town a short hike from the French border.

Little is known of Francese. Giorgio Vasari does not mention him in his *Lives of the Artists*, but a librarian at the University of Padua has published a private letter that does. She believes the letter, addressed to the Duchess of Ferrara, was "almost certainly" written by Vasari. It alludes to a notable portrait "*eseguito da Pietro Francese*" of one of the Duchess's nephews. André Benefiel wrote briefly about Pierre de Varenna in his 1661 treatise, *Les Peintres du Grand Siècle.* Here is the passage in its entirety:

Maître Pierre de Varenna was much admired, especially for his portraits.

He did not paint in the grand style, depicting the mythological

and pious subjects popular at the time, especially in the Catholic

provinces, where he was known as Pietro Francese. In some respects, his work has much in common with the painting being done today in the Low Countries. He produced remarkable portraits and scenes from everyday life, always on small canvases. It was the inner truth of his portraits his contemporaries found most worthy of praise. Francesco Della Rovere, Duke of Urbino, said of him, "*Altri artisti dipingono dall'esterno verso l'interno, ma questo Francese dipinge dall'interno verso l'esterno.*" (Other artists paint from the outside in, but this Francese paints from the inside out.)

Francese did not sign his work, perhaps out of humility, or *ad majoram gloria Dei*, like the artists of the Middle Ages. As a consequence, identifying, let alone cataloguing, his works has been almost impossible. It is likely that his scenes of everyday life and penetrating portraits hang unacknowledged on walls in houses great and small, in provincial museums designated *Pictor Ignotus*, and one in a sixteen-square-meter room of the modest house in Ventimiglia. The building was owned by an old widow who rented rooms to vacationers, save for the one in which she lived out her life. This woman claimed to be a descendant of a minor branch of the D'Este family. Her will bequeathed the house to the state with the provision that her room would become a museum to display her most prized possession, a family heirloom.

The museum's one exhibit is an eight-by-ten-centimeter detail from a study for a portrait of a young woman and not even all of that, as the paper has been torn. It shows only the left side of the unidentified woman's face. Still, the tiny museum has attracted some attention, and the enigmatic face never fails to evoke a response. The Visitors' Book includes not only the names of vacationers who stopped by on rainy afternoons but also those of professors and painters. Many of these people recorded their impressions of what they saw in the picture. Here is a list: beauty about to bloom, a repressed nature, a tease, determination, anxiety, pride, lasciviousness, piety, rebelliousness, sharp intelligence, placidity, chastity, fortitude, vanity, submissiveness, melancholy, modesty, earnestness, a quick wit, a passionate nature. Of these comments, the longest and most memorable is that of the Post-Impressionist painter, Marie Serrurier, who wrote "*c'est une muse évidemment aimée de l'artiste*"—a muse manifestly beloved by the artist.

2. *Le Musée des Armes Ratées - marche comique en si bémol mineur et do dièse majeur, pour orchestre militaire désaccordé, dissonant, cacophane, et maladroit*

Albert Hugo, Comte de Roanne and Captaine d'Infanterie, and Laurent Vagaray, Caporal and former miner, survived the Battle of Verdun, though narrowly. The Comte had pulled Vagaray from under the heavy clods thrown up by a German shell from a Feldhaubitze. Four nights later, Vagaray returned the favor. He shot dead one of a squad of infiltrators who had slipped into their trench and was about to bayonet the sleeping captain. All the veterans of the hyper-battle shared a bond but the one between Albert and Laurent was stronger than most. Moreover, both were embittered by the stupidity and slaughter they had witnessed and endured.

After the war, the Comte, whose family had considerable wealth in land and investments, loaned Vagaray the money to set up a scrap metal business in Rioges, on the same side of the Loire as Roanne. Vagaray had married before the war. When the Comte wed in 1919, he asked Vagaray to serve as best man, which put the long noses of his snobbish family out of joint.

In 1920, Charles Ginistry, Bishop of Verdun, initiated the project to erect the Douamont Ossuary by the vast National Necropolis. The land around of Verdun was a city of the dead, but the bishop wanted to make a monument of the physical remains of bloodletting on both sides. The Battle of Verdun lasted nearly a year; tens of millions of shells were fired. There were 800,000 casualties.

A year later, on a Sunday morning, the Comte sat across from his friend at the Vigaray family table in Rioges, two pacifists missing mass which Celeste Vigaray and her children were attending, as was the Comte's bride, Marie-Charlotte. They discussed the Ossuary about which they had mixed feelings.

"It won't do to pile up bones, let alone to tell people war is the worst of pestilences. It won't even do to show them the skeletons and the crosses," said Albert. "So long as war is seen as evil, it won't lose its fascination. The murderousness will always be turned into honor, glory, patriotism, extolled as heroic sacrifice, as if anybody wanted to be blown to bits or shredded by machine guns."

"That's true," said Laurent, nodding. "I shudder whenever they call me a hero. You?"

"I just want to spit."

"That Bishop of Verdun is a good man and so is his intention, I'm sure. He's already raising a good deal of money for his Ossuary. German skeletons will be piled in with ours. I like that."

"So do I. But I doubt it will do any real good."

"If displaying 130,000 skulls and pelvises isn't enough, what is?"

"*Ridicule*," said Albert.

"What?"

"There's no glory in what's laughable, Laurent, and no one's going to laugh at the dead."

Vigaray put down his bowl of coffee and looked closely at his friend. "You've been hatching some idea. You look just as you did when you insisted on helping me to set up my business. So, what have you got in mind?"

"I want to do as the Bishop is doing. I want to set up a memorial, and I also want it there, in Verdun. I have my eye on some land in Thierville. It's less than three kilometers from the city. Maybe those who come to mourn will make a short detour to laugh."

"No offense, Albert, but it sounds absurd."

"Absurd? Yes, that's just the point."

"And you want my help? I'm no comedian."

"No, but your business has flourished; you've got connections. I think you can help me assemble the exhibits."

"Exhibits? For what?"

"I'll be giving you a list."

It took a couple of years and thousands of francs, but, between them, Albert and Laurent managed to gather, among others, the following items.

1.The MacAdam Shield Spade. The idea here was to make an entrenching tool that would double as a defense against high-velocity bullets. The thick steel had a hole in it through which a rifle could be aimed. The thing proved too heavy to wield, the blade too blunt to serve as an effective spade, and, of course, it had a hole in it.

2.The Chatuchat Light Machine Gun. This was arguably the worst of all the failed weapons fielded by any side in the war. It was designed to be cheaply made, with thin metal parts that often snapped. The joints were poorly fashioned and let in dirt and sand. The fragile barrel quickly overheated; its semi-circular magazine regularly jammed and, from time to time, the gun simply disintegrated.

3.The Comte managed to get hold of an early pursuit plane of the type that first mounted a machine gun behind the propeller. This was before synchronization was perfected, so the propeller was invariably shot off.

4.Equally useless, and nearly as fatal to the pilot, was a Bréguet XIV fitted with a ten-meter spike bolted to the top wing that was supposed to bring down balloons and zeppelins by popping them.

5.The Mobile Personnel Protector was another misbegotten attempt to shield advancing infantry. It resembled an oversized trash collector and was to be pushed from behind. It had just enough room for four small soldiers inside and was made of iron as were its two oversized wheels. It proved too heavy to lift out of the trenches and, even when this was achieved, the contraption was nearly impossible to move. It turned over on anything but flat ground of which, of course, there was none among the craters of No Man's Land.

6.By far the largest item in the museum was the Paris gun, obtained at a bargain price by Laurent through connections in inflation-ridden Germany. It was designed to propel large shells over unprecedented distances, all the way from the Front to Paris—thus, the name. But it seldom hit its targets because each round fired distorted the extended barrel, quickly making trajectories so inaccurate as to be virtually random.

Le Musée des Armes Ratées opened to the public in 1925 and enjoyed some success. German as well as French veterans brought their families. The former combatants' responses were generally grim and sardonic, but their children laughed and were fascinated. The boys would gather together and earnestly exchange views on how the armaments could have been improved and dreaming up new weapons, fantastical ideas like death rays but also ones that seemed too plausible, like bombs crammed with germs that would wipe out people and spare buildings.

The decision to close down the museum was reached in January 1933. The Comte's hope that a display of moronic and unworkable weaponry would serve as an effective metaphor had worn away by then. The veterans no longer visited, nor did women; but young men came in numbers, as if to an amusement park. They were too young to have experienced the trenches; they knew only the speeches, the pride of fathers and uncles, the expurgated history. Those who took no lesson from the amputees on the streets and the blind in the Métro would not learn it from a shovel with a hole in it. The weapons that didn't work made them think of those that did—the artillery, machine guns, airplanes. What was once lethal now seemed to them beautiful. They spoke of tanks as though they were toys, of guns as if they were made to spurt water rather than lead. The young visitors from Germany—neatly pressed and stiff—exchanged nods and knowing smiles.

The decision to shut the museum was made on a Sunday evening. The Comte had invited the Vigarays to supper. The wives were now old friends, and Albert's son Georges loved being around Laurent's older children. Everyone had enjoyed a hearty winter's dinner of lamb roasted with carrots, parsnips, and potatoes with braised sprouts for the green. The wine was a sturdy burgundy. Afterwards, the women gossiped, the children went upstairs to play, and the two men repaired to Albert's paneled study where, with grunts they didn't used to make, they sank into matching red leather club chairs.

Pouring cognac into a pair of snifters, Albert said, "You see what's going to happen, don't you?"

"I'm afraid so," Laurent replied gloomily. "All the old business again. Dreams of adulation, swooning women. Loving the country in the wrong way. I really believed—?"

"Didn't we all?"

"Never again, we said. Not possible, we said. But then I imagine that's what people say at the end of even little, ordinary wars."

Albert got to his feet with a grunt, crossed to a cabinet, opened the bottom drawer, and returned with a book bound in tin, heavily dented.

"What's that?" asked Laurent.

"You don't remember? We took from that dead German, the one who looked to be about seventeen."

"Oh yes. So, you kept it. I don't read German. What's in it?"

"Dangerous nonsense, just the kind to turn the empty heads of thoughtless youngsters. The Boche General Staff had this book distributed to all their troops. It was written by a philosopher who'd been dead sixteen years by the time of Verdun, though I don't think that excuses him. Listen: *Man hat auf das große Leben verzichtet, wenn man auf den Krieg verzichtet.*"

"Which means?"

"Who has renounced war has also renounced greatness. It was, I see now, a ridiculous notion, jeering war out of existence."

"Maybe war's like love? I mean, it always finds a way."

"Hmpf. Well, they do say all's fair in both, meaning neither is fair at all. Farce and rape, invasion and seduction, skirmish and frontal assault. But it's not just that people didn't know or forget, Laurent. It's the allure, the exaltation, the downright sexiness. It's the beauty of a pursuit plane in flight or a star shell going off at night. It's the comradeship, girls, proud parents, the neighbors. It's every stupid enticement I hoped we could laugh into oblivion. It's that mad philosopher's idea of 'the great life.'"

After this defeatist speech the men fell silent.

"The tanks are much improved," said Laurent at length. "They have turrets now. And they say the artillery's much better too."

"But the airplanes most of all. I'm closing our little museum, Laurent. You were right to call it absurd. You can sell the exhibits for scrap. I think they'll be turned back into weapons soon enough."

"God forbid!"

"It's shameful to laugh so near to the dead. It was folly to try to thumb our noses in the shadow of that Ossuary's tower and the National Cemetery. Such things shouldn't be mocked, can't be—and they can't be intimidated either."

"But they can be expanded."

"Alas, yes. And next time the weapons will be still stupider—especially the ones that work."

3. *Le Musée des Guides de Conversation – sonatine pour deux flûtes déplacées et harpe en ut majeur, désinvolte, péripatéticienne, polyglotte et insipide*

The Johanssons were childless mid-century Americans. They met when Hannah, up till then a city girl, applied to and was accepted by Pittsburg State University which her mother assumed was in Pennsylvania. George, a native Kansan, was in Pittsburg to study agronomics. After some hesitation, Hannah chose to major in, of all things, French. They met at a mixer, hit it off, and married right after graduation. Hannah adjusted to her new life on the farm passed on to George by his parents, who inherited the land from George's grandfather, who was bequeathed it by George's great-grandfather, a Swedish immigrant who acquired the 160 acres allowed by the Homestead Act once the Civil War wrapped up and the Arapaho, Cheyenne, Comanche, Kansa, Kiowa, Osage, Pawnee, and Wichita were elbowed aside.

The Johanssons' land produced corn and soybeans, usually in abundance, but the crops came with worries about drought, hail, tornadoes, the cost of fertilizer, repairs, pesticides, what Congress' latest farm bill would say, and the all-important price per bushel. The farm had some cows and chickens too, but it was chiefly just fields of corn and soybeans in the flattest part of Kansas. Most years the Johanssons turned a moderate profit, more than a short-order cook would make but less than a truck driver.

Hannah had an Uncle Jules, childless like herself. He had been exceptionally close to his older sister, Hannah's mother, who pretty much raised him. Unlike their parents, she was unfazed by his homosexuality. In fact, she identified it before he did.

During the war, Jules worked at the Brooklyn Navy Yard, and he met a lot of sailors. He partnered with one in both the personal and business sense, a savvy go-getter from the Bronx. After the war, they pooled their savings to buy a tract of land on Long Island, where, with some almost unimpeachably legal financing, they built thirty-five cheap and identical houses. They took a portion of the profits and bought an apartment in Brooklyn Heights. As a man of property, Jules made a will, leaving all his assets to his sister or, should she God forbid predecease him, her children. A year later, Jules and his partner bought land in Westchester County where they erected fewer but far more expensive homes, fake Tudors and Dutch colonials. When Jules died three years after his partner and one year after his sister, Hannah was surprised to learn that the uncle she hadn't seen in two decades had made a mint and invested it wisely.

The New York lawyer who was Jules' executor sent Hannah a certified letter and followed up with a phone call. He explained everything and saw to all the arrangements. And this is how the Johanssons came into money, a staggering sum by their standards.

"It's yours," said George to Hannah. "What do you want to do with it?"

Hannah didn't hesitate. "We'll keep the farm, of course. It's our home; it's your family legacy and I've been content here. But what I've always longed to do is travel—I want to go to France and Italy and, well, everywhere."

George felt a little hurt. He had long before persuaded himself that his formerly urban wife loved living on a farm in the middle of America. "You never said."

"No point." Over the years, Hannah had become as laconic as her spouse.

The plan was to take four trips a year, one per season. This was at the end of the 1950s when Boeing's 707 initiated the Jet Age. In those days, people dressed up to go to airports and dressed even more up if they were flying. It was the time when American tourists became an important entry on the balance sheets of countries still recovering from the war and when few of their citizens, even the hotel clerks, sales personnel, and waiters spoke English. It was a boom time for guidebooks and bilingual tour guides.

The first trip was, of course, to Paris in April not just because of Hannah's exotic college major but also because of the song. They spent two weeks in the capital and one more in Nice exploring the Riviera. George bought a Leica and took loads of pictures. Back home, he bought a Kodak slide projector and had his rolls of film made into slides they could show friends and neighbors. The Johanssons threw a party for the purpose. The friends and neighbors sat in polite silence through the hour-long display of George's snapshots and Hannah's running commentary. The barbecue afterwards was, by contrast, a smash hit.

The couple's second journey was in January, a week and a half in Germany and four days in Vienna. In June, they did Italy. The friends and neighbors invited in after these junkets kept their reluctance to themselves and most.

Fred and Gert Schultz always came for the slide shows, and even brought their three children though, like everybody else, they found the things tedious. But, after enduring slides of Rome, Florence, and Venice, Gert noticed the little stack of phrasebooks on the mantelpiece. She opened the one on top to a random page. It was the "Shopping" section.

"*Vorrei vedere delle scarpe*," she read haltingly but out loud.

"What's that?" Fred asked.

"It means 'I would like to see some shoes.'"

Fred held out his hand. "Let's see."

He paged to the section devoted to "Eating and Drinking" and read *Cameriere la lista, per favore*. He read it badly but with delight.

"How's that?" asked Sam Ritter who overheard.

"It means 'Waiter, the menu, please,' Sam."

"In what?"

"Italian."

"You speak Italian?"

"No. Look, it's from this book they took along with them."

Fred read another sentence, and with gusto. "*Mi porti un po' di caffé, adesso*. That's cup of joe, pronto."

Sam asked to see the paperback, took a look, laughed, and read out, *Per favore mostrami un reggiseno*. "Not one I'd need. Please show me a brassiere."

Drawn by the good cheer, others came over and picked up other books.

Harold Walker read, "*À quelle heure le diner est-il servi dans cet hotel*? What time can a guy get fed in this place?"

His wife Jeannette picked up the German phrasebook, turned a few pages. "Ha!" she exclaimed. "Listen to this: *Wann wird in diesen Hotel das Abendessen serviert?* It means *exactly* the same thing!"

Pictures of George sweating in front of the Bridge of Sighs, Hannah grinning outside the Sorbonne archway, both of them looking serious under the statue of Beethoven—all these failed to engage their stolid Kansas neighbors. It was no different with the records of later trips, like the picture of the two of them looking spectacularly out-of-place in front of the forty-one-meter reclining Buddha in Fukuoka. George explained it was taken by a giggling and obliging young woman in a kimono. "Maybe," he said daringly, "she was a geisha."

It was the phrasebooks that people liked. They had fun pronouncing the phonetic spellings and working out how many of the identical phrases turned up in all the books—how to ask for a brassiere, for instance. Reading the phrases out loud made them feel sophisticated and provincial at the same time, and pleased to be both.

The Johanssons traveled the world, but the returns diminished. All the airports resembled each other, as did the new hotels designed expressly for them. There were big tour groups in air-conditioned buses. The hotels served hamburgers and fries and Coca-Cola. Everywhere grew crowded and the tourists didn't care how they dressed. The Johanssons dutifully took in the sights the guidebooks said they ought to, ate what was recommended as local specialties, but they had scarcely any interesting interactions with local people. Every communication was mediated by the phrasebooks which they toted everywhere, just as people now do their cellphones.

The Johanssons kept the farm, but George left three of his four fields fallow. Eventually, they gave up both planting and their travels. They bought a condo in Coral Gables for the winters. George had the idea of turning their Kansas living room into a kind of monument to their wanderings, of which he was proud. He picked out his favorite photos, had them blown up, framed, and hung them on the walls with lengthy typed labels. Hannah laid out all their guidebooks and maps in neat geographical order. But the chief attraction even for the landlocked, isolationist, parochial, and self-satisfied remained the pile of phrasebooks. Over time, grownups no longer visited but their adolescent children did. They read to each other in all the languages with bright-eyed hilarity.

The phrases—*Where is the bathroom? How far are we from the river? May I have more sugar?*—struck them as banal but also exotic. They took to calling the old Johansson place The Phrasebook Museum, and it filled those pre-globalist, farm-bred teenagers with intoxicating dreams of adventure, liberation, and escape.

Petite Suite de Musiciens

1. *Instrumentalistes: Concerto helvétique en mi-majeur pour quatre mains et petit orchestre – anxieux, avec dix grammes de suspense, mais tout à fait charmant et pas du tout politique*

The Swiss resort town of Braunwald has held a Music Week every year since 1936, an amateur affair. To get on the cultural map and draw more summer tourists, the Town Council voted to hold a piano competition as the highlight of the Week. Initially, it was to be called the Braunwald Piano Competition but then Frau Bock, the most punctilious member of the Council as well as the town's official historian, pointed out that it is customary for such competitions to be named for distinguished musicians, such as the Cliburn, Chopin, and Tchaikovsky. She proposed that Braunwald's be called the Gieseking because Walter Gieseking had held master classes in the town back in 1944. The proposal provoked some controversy. Councilor Weber, who also knew some history, objected that both Vladimir Horowitz and Artur Rubinstein were on record calling Walter Gieseking a committed Nazi. The proposal was tabled without a vote and the meeting adjourned. Advised by Frau Bock, the Chairman of the Council, Herr Keller, addressed the issue at the next meeting. "As Frau Bock has observed, Gieseking didn't play Ravel or Debussy like a Nazi. What's more, he was born in Lyon. Frau Bock has shown me Gieseking's daughter's statement that her father was appalled by the Nazis and that the family would certainly have remained in Switzerland in 1944 had her mother not insisted on returning to Germany to care for her parents. No one questions Gieseking's musicianship," Keller declared, "or his connection to Braunwald. I move that we call our competition after him." As the matter of the great pianist's politics was deemed unresolvable, the majority decided they be set aside in the Swiss manner and Gieseking's name adopted.

Frau Bock was invited to head the competition's organizing committee which would formulate the rules, secure a distinguished panel of judges, and coordinate with the Music Week orchestra. She accepted the responsibility proudly and with her customary earnestness.

Contestants entering the First Annual Walter Gieseking Piano Competition had to be between the ages of fourteen and twenty-three. They were required to provide the Committee with three recommendations from professional musicians or prestigious academies along with a video not to exceed ten minutes in length. There would be three rounds with contenders eliminated after each. In the preliminary round, contestants would perform pieces from a prescribed list, the recital not to exceed more than one hour in length. For the second round, the remaining contestants would perform the first movement of one of four Mozart concerti accompanied by the Music Week Orchestra. In the final round, the finalists would perform a recital of works of their own choice.

Though Braunwald undertook to house and feed accepted entrants, they would have to provide for their own transportation. Getting seventeen-year-old Mylena Goraya and nineteen-year-old Yishai Maimon to Switzerland consumed the travel budget of both families. As the young people had no one else with whom to take in the sights and no money to shop or sample Braunwald's restaurants, Mylena and Yishai attended all the preliminary recitals. Each was sure the other was the best.

Meals were in the cafeteria of the Schulhaus. Mylena was shy but not Yishai. At dinner the night before the announcement of those who made it to the second round, Yishai, as usual, took his tray and sat next to Mylena.

"You played the Schumann so movingly," he said, "and the Bach inventions—*perfect*!"

Mylena blushed. In a soft, heavily accented voice she, replied, "You were better."

They chatted through dinner and then went for a stroll around the town. They spoke about their favorite pianists, about their teachers, and about Braunwald.

"Odd to call the town that," said Yishai. "Brown forest—as though all the trees had burnt."

"Maybe it's like Schwartzwald. Do you think brown, like black, just means dense?"

"I suppose. Probably not named after the shirts."

"The shirts?"

They told each other about their families. Yishai explained that his grandparents had left the Soviet Union for Israel in the wave of Jewish emigration in the 1980s. Two years earlier, his father had been injured in a terrorist explosion. His mother took care of him and worked full time for an insurance company. "I wanted to quit school and help, but Mother wouldn't hear of it. She insisted I go on with my studies." Mylena said her family left everything behind in Kiev after the Russian invasion and, through a relative of her mother, found refuge in Belgrade. "I had to get a special document from the government to be able to leave and return. Finding a piano to practice, food, pretending to be happy for my parents—it's hard," said Mylena. She made a sweeping gesture with her arm. "This place does not seem quite real to me. For you?"

"The Swiss are prosperous and oblivious," said Yishai with some bitterness. "Everything's hygienic except the bank deposits. They have to import their poor."

"There are poor people here?"

"I think you have to look very closely, maybe at the end of the alleys."

Mylena laughed.

There was no romantic spark between the two, but they liked each other. That night Yishai felt less alone and Mylena less homesick.

The following morning, they learned that most of the contestants had been eliminated and that they were not. They congratulated each other.

“Which Mozart will you choose?”

“The one I prepared, of course. Just in case.”

“Me, too.”

That afternoon Yishai came into the practice room just as Mylena was finishing up. He was carrying a portfolio.

“I’m so happy to see you,” he said. Mylena blushed and gave him another smile.

“Let’s play something together,” he said. “It’ll be fun. I’ve brought along something for four hands. Here. He took out some sheet music from his portfolio. You know it?”

“Yes, of course.”

It was fun.

Only six players had made it to the Mozart round. The poker-faced panel—"the hanging judges" Yishai called them—eliminated four. Only Mylena and Yishai were left. One or the other would win the competition and the contract that was the real prize.

Neither felt pleased.

“I wish *I’d* been eliminated,” said Yishai gallantly.

“I *should* have been,” said Mylena, the perfectionist.

“I could resign, disqualify myself.”

Mylena frowned. “If you do, I will too.”

"I know! We'll ask the Committee to declare a draw. We'll *both* win—and you can have the contract."

"Why not you?"

"Because you're better. Also, you're from Kiev and I'm from Tel Aviv."

They asked to meet with Frau Bock. She would not countenance a tie. "The rules," she said sternly, "are clear. *Ein Gewinner.* One winner. Your recitals will be attended by the whole town. Everybody is looking forward to them, especially the tourists. So, you will *not* spoil things. Reporters from Zurich, Bern, and Geneva will be here. It's possible there will be three more from Germany and two from France. No, you must compete. Also, I need your programs by this three o'clock this afternoon. Now, go away and practice!"

Every seat in the hall was filled. People stood not only at the back but also in the aisles. The mood was good, full of anticipation. Frau Bock surveyed the auditorium with satisfaction. The programs had been printed on time. The more knowledgeable were discussing the choices. The judges sat silently together in the front row looking dour, each with a notebook and pen at the ready.

Mylena was to play first. There was applause when she entered. Two young people at the back unfurled a yellow and blue Ukrainian flag and shouted, "Glory to Ukraine!" Mylena was dressed in a velvet dress, dark green, the color you get by mixing yellow and blue.

She acknowledged the audience with two little nods and sat down at the Bechstein. The hall grew quiet, awaiting the first chords of Chopin's First Ballade. She remained still for the few seconds it took Yishai to jump up from his seat and dash on to the stage. He wore a tuxedo with tails and a white kippah. He seated himself next to Mylena and laid out the sheet music.

A furious Frau Bock was on her feet and stomping toward the stage when Mylena and Yishai launched into their memorable, exuberant performance of the Franco-Brazilian *Scaramouche* composed by the Jewish refugee Darius Milhaud seven years before Walter Gieseking left Braunwald for Germany.

Then Mylena began a Scarlatti sonata, raised her hands, and Yishai finished it, launching at once into the first movement of Beethoven's *Waldstein* Sonata which Mylena completed. Then with a smile, they played Debussy's four-handed *En Blanc et Noir.*

The performance delighted the audience, who rose to their feet and clapped rhythmically while chanting *Beide! Beide!* The judges took the hint and declared the competition a tie. The chief judge suggested they flip a Swiss France to determine who got the prize and the contract. But the performance was so highly praised in the press that the young musicians were offered a much larger contract to perform as a duo. Everybody was pleased save for Frau Bock.

2. *Chef d'Orchestre: Concertino en si bémol mineur pour alto et orchestre de chambre - entiché, ennuyeux, et ironique un peu comme le châtiment de Tantale*

The internationally celebrated conductor, Johannes von Eitelmann, would have scoffed at the suggestion that he was an addict. He drank little and only to be sociable; he had a horror of drugs, even aspirin; he was monogamous during his two marriages, serially thereafter. His self-discipline was legendary, his capacity for work a source of astonishment. Tall, commanding, handsome, and gifted, he had been a success from his first appearance with the Mozarteum in Salzburg after just turning twenty. Had somebody proposed that he was addicted to music, he might have cordially agreed, but with an ironic smile.

Von Eitelmann was much in demand. He seldom declined an invitation to serve as guest conductor and, in summer, flitted from festival to festival—all in addition to serving as music director of two orchestras in two countries on two continents. People thought him a dedicated workaholic, but it wasn't work to which he was addicted, or even music. What lay behind his packed schedule and ubiquity was an insatiable craving for acclaim. He couldn't long go without applause thickly salted with bravos. He needed the approving bows and thumb-ups from concertmasters, the fulsome reviews of critics, the deference of peers, the respectful bows of old men and, still more, the fawning of young women.

Von Eitelmann was married young, to an oboist. Helene was still a student and the glamor of the young conductor, already with a name, was as attractive as his good looks and avid pursuit of her. All this outweighed her parents' doubts, their argument that she was too young and so, for that matter, was Johannes. Helene had no doubts. She was in love and also in awe. Von Eitelmann drank his wife's admiration as Dracula might have her blood and, in only a year and a half, Helene found that she was drained.

Von Eitelmann's second marriage, four years later, was to Leonie Hübsch, the favorite niece of the Austrian foreign minister. By then, he was under contract to the Philharmonic. The wedding was the social event of the year in Vienna. The guests included the president of the republic, a throng of ministers, ambassadors, famous soloists, and a good chunk of the diplomatic corps.

Leonie was well educated, cosmopolitan and, at the start, adored the man she playfully called "*Maestro Mio*." However, under the unrelenting pressure to admire him, her husband's frequent absences, and their quarrels about having the children for whom she longed and he emphatically did not, the marriage foundered. Leonie's adoration evaporated and *suo maestro*

turned sarcastic. The divorce, unlike the wedding, was a quiet affair. Publicity was unavoidable, but it was at least discreet. The couple was described as saddened by their decision to separate and the break was diplomatically described as amicable.

For the next three years, Johannes indulged in three liaisons when his crammed schedule permitted. The women were all star-struck music-lovers attracted by his fame. They flattered him and were, in turn, flattered by his attentions. But, when the stars dimmed and the flattery stopped, Johannes shrugged and moved on.

Grace Kronbach's mother dragged her to the concert at the Academy of Music in Philadelphia through which she yawned, diverting herself by looking up random phrases on her smartphone. She learned that *occasions of sin* is credited to Saint Bernardine, a canonized misogynist and anti-Semite. *Man is the only animal that blushes—or needs to.* She had been pretty sure that was Mark Twain, and it was. *Should I kill myself, or have a cup of coffee?* She'd heard that line from her depressive friend Andrea, but it sounded like a quotation. And so it was, attributed to Albert Camus, but probably made up by some wag summarizing *The Myth of Sisyphus*. Who said *The universe is a big place, perhaps the biggest*? Kurt Vonnegut. She giggled. "Shh," said her mother scowling at Grace and looked daggers at her phone.

Mrs. Kronbach was only a little more interested in the benefit concert than her daughter. She was really there for the reception. As a member of the board of WOMEN HELPING WOMEN she needed to see and be seen. She got her daughter to come with her not only because her philistine husband flatly refused to, but so that she too would be seen. In her mother's opinion, Grace didn't mix enough, at least not with the best society.

The program was all-female: Germaine Tailleferre's *Concertino for Harp and Orchestra*, Cecile Chaminade's *Concertino for Flute and Orchestra*, Fanny Mendelssohn's *Overture in C-major*, and, to conclude, Clara Schumann's *Piano Concerto*. The soloists were all women too, well-known professionals performing *pro bono*. The event attracted a lot of attention when it was announced that Johannes Von Eitelmann had consented to come down from New York, where he had just finished a stint conducting *La Forza del Destino* at the Metropolitan Opera.

The catered reception was mobbed. The room was barely large enough for the food and the freshly-coiffed members of WOMEN HELPING WOMEN and their guests. Mrs. Kronbach surveyed the crowd, nodded and smiled at her fellow board members, then took Grace by the elbow and more or less dragged her to the receiving line waiting to thank and congratulate the great conductor.

"He's very handsome," she whispered, "even better-looking up close. Don't you think?"

Grace said nothing. She was looking across the room at a woman in a rather ridiculous dress the color of a rotting plum.

Johannes shook Mrs. Kronbach's offered hand and thanked her for her compliments. But his eyes were fastened on Grace. Not since the young oboist had he felt such an erotic shock. He took her in—face, figure, eyes, hair. Perhaps because of Tailleferre and Chaminade, the phrase *coup de foudre* came into his head. *Les mots tout à juste.* The maestro was well and truly smitten.

"Did you enjoy the program?" he asked Grace.

"Some of the songs were nice," she said. "I don't really care for classical music."

"Songs?"

"Grace calls everything songs," said Mrs. Kronbach quickly. "It's exasperating. Her little brother got all the musical talent. Bradley plays the trombone."

Johannes canceled his next engagement then the one after that. He asked Grace to an all-Chopin recital by Lang Lang. Her mother insisted that she accept. Grace was not impressed. In fact, she wanted to leave after the intermission, though she allowed that the pianist's name was cute.

He asked her to go to dinner with him. She suggested a restaurant at which, according to Andrea, it was impossible to get a reservation.

He got one. Over the *haute cuisine* he talked only a little about himself, saying he wanted to find out what interested her. Grace said she was curious about a newly translated German play she'd heard the University's Drama Club was putting on. "But apparently the only performance is sold out." Johannes got tickets. The theater was exiguous, overheated, and smelled bad, the play relentlessly depressing and poorly acted. Grace liked it. She said it reminded her of Kafka's "In the Penal Colony." Johannes had heard of Kafka but had not read "In the Penal Colony."

Von Eitelmann struggled to put Grace Kronbach out of his mind, to achieve an indifference that would match hers, to forget her. He failed. When she agreed to meet him for coffee, he implored her to come with him to Vienna. "I'll be conducting my reconstruction of Mahler's *Tenth*. I would love to have you at the performance."

Grace put down her fork, looked at him with surprise, then shrugged. "But why would I do that?"

Back in Vienna for the Mahler, Von Eitelmann got his first bad review.

3. *Compositeur: La Muse Infantile - thème et variations limitées en si-mineur pour basson et orchestre de soutien sous la forme d'un pneu crevé*

"You're sure you're okay with this?"

"I can manage it."

"You want me to show you how the diaper works again?"

"Nope. It's been a while, but I've changed diapers—my stinky nephew's. Not a problem. What I want is for the two of you to go, have a great time and not worry."

Julia looked dubious, hesitant, but also eager and provisionally grateful. From what I knew of her husband the Patriots fan, respite care must be a blue-moon event. She and Barb, her only sister and my only helpmate, hadn't seen each other since just after the baby was born. But they talked almost daily, and Barb could tell Julia needed a break. She asked her to come with the baby for the weekend. She had a shopping list and a romcom she'd like to see. Barb would be getting a respite, too.

"I guess he can handle a diaper, even if he's useless as a composer," she said making it sound like a joke, as if I weren't useless.

Julia changed the subject. "I'll feed Autumn. She always goes down right after."

Autumn. An unusual name, but a good one, pretty but serious.

"It's because she was born on the twenty-second, first day of Fall. She came with the equinox," Julia had explained on our postpartum visit to adore the infant.

"I think it's nice," Barb said, "and there won't be a lot of other Autumns in her classes. There were always about *ten* other Barbaras in mine."

Julia reviewed the paraphernalia with me three times. The bottle. The diapers. The little stuffed dromedary. The pacifier. The collapsible playpen. The infant seat.

"You probably won't need most of it."

"Check," I said.

When Julia declared the baby officially down, the sisters left, giggling like schoolgirls even before the door shut behind them.

My parents were less than pleased that I went to a university that turned out captains of industry, precocious entrepreneurs, lawyers, doctors, bankers, and members of Congress but chose music as my major. They regarded my piano playing and the little pieces I wrote in my early years as tolerable hobbies for a teenager, not a career for a grown-up who might want to live in the middle class. "Composing isn't a livelihood," they said. The composers they could name had all been dead for a long time.

Barbara didn't agree with them. When we were married, she encouraged my artistic ambition and maybe that was part of my attraction for her. After all, her own major had been art history. But, after a few years of failure, blockage, frustration, and short money, she more or less adopted the view of Mom and Dad.

My day job at the time was operating a forklift for the Donnelly Manufacturing Company, part-time. It paid less than Barb's bookkeeping gig and that didn't pay much.

"Tell me again why you can't get a proper job," she said one night in bed.

"You really want me to say it again?"

"Oh, right," she said bitingly. "It's because you need the time for composing." She made an unpleasant noise, turned out the light and her back on me.

Autumn slept for maybe an hour. I was in the living room, stalking the spinet, waiting for a phrase, an interval, anything that might have traction. I did that a lot. I hadn't written anything in months and not very much before that. Would I have sold my soul for a leitmotif? Maybe, but nobody offered.

Barbara was hinting at divorce. Two days before she had said, "Maybe you'd do better if I weren't here. Maybe I would, too. You know?" I fantasized about her moving in with my parents so they could enjoy long evenings trashing me en-masse. I had a notion that leaving me with her infant niece might have been a hint. Not only should I give up musical composition and forklifts, but I ought to make her pregnant and get a proper job. My parents would love that, especially if the grandchild came with an office.

Autumn was in the bedroom. Julia had laid her down in the play pen on a little mattress with a pair of rolled-up pink blankets hemming her in. She was crying but it sounded more like a demand for company than distress. When she saw me, she smiled and put out her little arms. I picked her up carefully. She hugged my neck.

"Would you like to hear a joke? Well, a riddle, actually," I said to her angelic face. "Yes? Well then, what's the difference between a composer and a large pepperoni pizza? You don't know? The pizza can feed a family of four."

She giggled just as if she got it.

We went on a tour of the kitchen then the living room. Autumn pointed at the spinet. Holding her to my chest with my right arm, I picked out a little of Ravel's left-handed piano concerto. She made an approving noise.

I found the infant seat, put it down on the floor beside the piano, and laid her in it. That was when we locked eyes.

Have you ever noticed that some infants have this weirdly wise expression, as if they know something terribly important they haven't yet forgotten but you have? Well, it might just have been gas, but that was the look Autumn gave me. It felt encouraging, comforting. Here at last, I thought, was someone who believed in me.

She began to babble. I imitated her noises back at her. Then I sat down and played them on the piano. She loved that. She'd babble whole notes, half-notes, quarter-notes—then wait for me to play them. She squealed and babbled some more, and I played them back. I couldn't say which of us was more enchanted.

I found a piece of paper, drew in the lines, and wrote down what

Autumn prattled and what I played. When she tired of the game and dozed off, I left her in the infant seat and started playing with the notes. I found a theme, a promising, generative sort of tune—lovely, light, simple but also pregnant. I played it softly, looked down on the sleeping infant and whispered, "Bless you, child." Then I fetched her dromedary and laid it next to her.

Over the next week, I made a set of variations on the theme. I wrote them one after another at a speed I'd never before attained. Barb liked the piece, though she complained about my playing late into the night. But, above all, she was amazed to see her husband, that futile and feckless figure of futility, filling pages of sheet music so quickly.

The music came easily, the way I've heard some women describe a second birth. *Autumn, Theme and Variations* was completed in ten busy days, nine inspired nights.

The first variation was a sunny portrait of baby Autumn. Next came a march for the return to school, then a harvest minuet, an impressionist rendering of colorful leaves, a variation for the Jewish holidays with an obligato that sounded like a Klezmer clarinet. I made a jagged variation to represent high-school anxiety and a sweet one for budding hormonal romances. The final variation was seasonal too, autumnal melancholy in a mournful slow and gentle minor. It was all good.

I was exhausted in absolutely the best sense, like a salmon who had fought a river, climbed a dam, dodged grizzlies, made it home and spawned. Even Barb was provisionally impressed. "It's the best thing you've done," she admitted. "For your sake, I hope there's more to come."

I sent an email to Professor Cromwell, the one teacher at the Institute who had encouraged me. I told him I thought I'd made a breakthrough and described the piece. He wrote back that he was glad to hear from me and offered to get together the following Tuesday afternoon.

We met in his office then went to a basement practice room. I played *Autumn* for him, all of it. He was enthusiastic. “Bravo!” he exclaimed tapping his fingers together by way of applause. And he did more than that.

“Look, I know the music director of the Symphony. We’re old friends. Fred’s always on the lookout for new work to premiere, especially by somebody local. New—but not *too* new, of course. You know what I mean. Premieres are rare. They’re not what subscribers subscribe for. Your piece is tuneful, accessible, yet contemporary. May I make a suggestion?”

I was beaming. “Of course.”

“Orchestrate it and I’ll make sure it gets to Fred.”

“Wonderful! Of course I’ll do it.”

“Good. Let me know when it’s ready. I happen to know they’ve left a slot open for the final concert and your variations might fill it. Work hard and don’t dawdle.”

I did work hard. I did the orchestration in a month. It was fun, the way work ought to be. Professor Cromwell was as good as his word. Friedrich Böhm agreed to look at the score. He said that would be sufficient. He didn’t need to hear it.

Autumn led off the final program of the season. Barbara bought a purple dress. My parents came. The piece was a hit. The critics were almost excessively generous with their praise. It was performed in Cleveland and San Francisco the next season. I was called up on stage on both occasions. I accepted two commissions and said farewell to the forklift.

Then. . . nothing. The salmon went belly up in the water. I sat at the piano. I stared at the paper. I started and stopped. I tore up a lot of sheet music. Barbara complained about our bank account. “Blocked again today?" That was how she greeted me when she got home from work.

My desperation swelled like a boil. Then I had an idea.

"Let's visit Julia this weekend," I said to Barb. "I'm sure the two of you would like to see each other. And maybe if I got away."

"Really? You think? Well, I can give her a call and see if she'll have us."

Of course, it wasn't Julia I wanted to see, or her football-loving spouse. It was Autumn.

She had grown. She was walking and even saying a few words. When Barb and I came into the house, she hid behind her mother and wouldn't look me in the eye. The wisdom had gone. The babbling was replaced by *Mommy*, *Daddy*, and especially *No*.

I still try once in a while, but less and less. The piano's out of tune, Barb is pregnant, and I work in insurance.

Inside the Pale

The tavern was overcrowded and overheated. An early spring and recent downpours made the air as muggy as if it were July instead of April. Everyone felt as if he were inhaling what everybody else was exhaling. The pickled cucumbers and vodka were warm too, though this discouraged no one. At first, the conversation was about planting but soon moved on to the usual grievances, gossip, resentments, petty feuds, and complaints about wives. It was an ordinary Tuesday evening. The peasants were working their way to drunkenness when Pyotr Stepanovich Nenanov suddenly burst through the swinging door. He was in a panic.

"Olesya's missing!"

Nenanov had been a man of no account, an unpopular landless laborer whose general attitude toward life was that the original sin was committed against him. But, four years earlier, he persuaded Igor Kirilenko's widow to marry him. Kirilenko had been a small-holder, and the widow needed a man to help with the farm. Nenanov tended to the chores and treated Masha decently. With Kirilenko's ten-year-old daughter Olesya, who missed her father far more than her mother did, he was patient, even tender. Those who predicted a catastrophe decided that it had proved a good match, after all.

"She went out to fetch the cow after dinner and didn't come back. Masha and I have been all over calling her name. Nothing!"

Nenanov looked around the smoky room with wild eyes then struck his fist on a table.

"*They* took her!"

Everybody knew who *they* were but also that Nenanov hated and feared them. He refused to set foot in Mukizma, their neighborhood, not even for a bowl of Bronicki's famous borscht and fresh rye bread.

"Calm down, Petya. She'll come home when she's ready," said one.

"Probably just daydreaming by the pond or off giggling somewhere with her friend Katya," said another.

"Don't you think we went to the pond? And Katya hasn't seen her since Sunday at church."

One peasant put down his glass and boomed out, "Could be she's with Simonov's boy."

There was general laughter.

But when Olesya's body was found the next day crudely buried in the wasteland just outside Mukizna things changed.

That night Nenanov was back in the tavern, haranguing the men.

"Masha's crying all the time. I'm losing my mind! I want revenge!"

"The police—" someone began.

Nenanov scoffed. "The police won't do anything, and they'll take two months doing it. I'm telling you it's up to us! It's April. Everybody knows that's when they slaughter innocent Christian children. Oh, the poor girl! My sweet little Olya! My daughter! Are you all cowards? I'm telling you we have to do what they did in Kishinev and Odessa."

"Petya's right. Cossacks are the only true Russians."

"And it's so. They *do* drink Christian blood at Easter, the vampires!"

One man stood. "Listen to me! We should get them Saturday. *This* Saturday. In the morning."

"That's smart, Sasha. They don't stir an elbow on Saturdays. We'll smash them in their beds or burn them in that shack they pray in."

"And we'll get the women, too."

"Especially the young ones!"

After that, they had another round of vodka, linked arms, and sang "Dark-Eyed Cossack Girl".

Lieutenant Besinsky got wind of what was brewing. He was friendly with Bronicki and sweet on his daughter, Basye. He went to Mukizma to warn his friend.

"We won't be able to stop them," he said somberly. "Hell, it'll be all I can do to keep my boys from joining them."

Yitzak Yakovivich Bronicki was a big man, clever, tough, brave, and not easily excited. He had thrown more than one drunken peasant out of his eatery. But there were only two days.

He thanked Besinsky then ran around Mukizma hammering on doors. By midnight, all the men and half the women were in the study house, the men downstairs, the women up.

"As you know, there's to be a pogrom on the Sabbath. That girl they found."

Consternation and wailing, fear and panic.

"Where can we run?"

"We can fight back!"

"You fool, against those peasants and their clubs?"

"They'll have horses and sabers, too."

"On the Sabbath! When we're forbidden to do anything!"

Bronicki calmly waited for people to calm down, then asked the rabbi to remind everyone about the Pikuach Nefesh, the obligation to preserve human life that trumps all other rules.

Pious old Shmuel Perkat tottered to his feet, held up a finger, and declared that, with respect to the rabbi, the Pikuach Nefesh applied only to saving a particular life.

"*Your* life is particular, Perkat. So is your Nekha's. And my Sosya's."

Perkat grumbled but sat down.

"What can we do but call on the Almighty?" said the rabbi and began intoning a prayer. "King of the Universe, deliver us! May You answer us on the day we call!"

Bronicki bowed his head and waited for the rabbi to finish. After the collective Ahmayn, he went from man to man, woman to woman, instructing everyone as to what they had to do and do quickly.

The peasants groggily approached the Mukizma district at eight o'clock Saturday morning. Some carried scythes and torches; most had clubs. All were hungover from the heavy drinking they had done the night before working themselves up into being a proper mob. They weren't making much noise; it was as if they didn't want to wake the Jews. Nenanov, who walked in the lead, felt this was wrong. They should be making a terrifying racket. He turned around and shouted Olesya's name then a string of terrible oaths. He tried beginning to sing the Cossack song but only two or three took up the tune. The men had stopped and were staring up at a banner unfurling between the gates of the ghetto. In tall Cyrillic letters, it read WELCOME TO JEWISH FESTIVAL MUKIZMA. Then a clarinet sounded a rising strain—half whine, half prayer—and a Klezmer band struck up "Dance, Dance, Bulgar". A dozen young men in white shirts and fur hats poured into the street and commenced kicking up their heels in unison, perhaps like Bulgars.

Even Nenanov gawped as a dozen young girls in flowered skirts and flowing hair joined hands began circling around the men, singing demurely.

Bronicki came forward with a broad grin and addressed the nonplused peasants loudly, almost in a voice of command.

"Brothers, so good of you to come! We were hoping you'd join us. Please, enter!"

And they did. There were booths and tables all up and down the street. There were all sorts of cakes and cookies, pickled tomatoes and herring, roasted chickens, apples and fried potatoes. The blacksmith was turning half a lamb on a spit next to a bin piled high with salted bagels. A violinist in a caftan scraped away merrily beside a quartet of singers. At the far end of the street stood a puppet theater and a tent with a teller of fortunes wearing a scarlet scarf around her head.

The peasants leaned their clubs on the ground. Some abandoned them entirely and reached for the stack of plates and glasses of sweetened tea and kvass. Sosya Bronicki stood behind a trestle table on which lay a huge pot of borscht, a large basin of sour cream, a stack of clay bowls, and a basket of warm rye loaves.

"What do you call this? It's good."

"Your Jew music is really lively."

"Hey, kike. Hand me a glass of that tea."

There was everything good, except vodka.

Was there no trouble at all? Impossible, but, by the time the sun set, only three shops had been looted, just one set on fire; only three men were beaten and just one lost an eye. Tsipa Nuchmar was dragged into an alley by a peasant called Tolya but was saved by a brute named Oleg who had a grudge against Tolya over some pastureland. He always carried a hammer in his belt. So Tolya's arm was broken and Tsipa made her escape.

The police investigation proceeded and, a month later, after he was found guilty of the rape and murder of his fourteen-year-old stepdaughter, Pyotr Stepanovich Nenanov was sent under guard to the prison camp at Nerchinsk.

The Ex-Consul

Harry Frager's final post was at the largest American consulate in Europe. The building looked like a hefty slice of the Pentagon. The place was always bustling, busy with the troubles of members of the military and their families, the entanglements and deaths of expatriates, businesspeople wanting help, the contretemps of reckless students and the arrests of boorish tourists. The Consul General, Frager's boss, was an oilman and a friend of the President's, a famous bundler; that is, a wealthy contributor who gathered up other rich contributors the way peasants used to sheaves. As Deputy Principal Officer, Frager saw to pretty much everything save for banquets and receptions. The Consul General prided himself on being from the Lone Star State, his Italian suits, his third wife, and what he called, with only the haziest irony, "my gift for delegation". Frager's career ended shortly after he imprudently let slip some candid remarks about the current Administration. In deference to his rank and years of service, he was given an extra day to clear out his desk. As he was doing so, the boss came by to deliver a cynical comment and a farewell present. "I'm surprised, Frager. I thought you were a professional diplomat." The gift was a cookbook called *No Mess Texas Cuisine.*

It was because of this book that Harry Frager inadvertently became a local hero.

Over his thirty-two-year career, Frager was seldom in the United States, a Thanksgiving here, a funeral there. During their marriage, his adventurous wife preferred they take their vacations in places like Borneo, Mongolia, and Lapland. Jeanne was a good ad for joi de vivre and some of that rubbed off on Frager, or rather it neutralized his melancholy tendencies.

An orphan, only child, and now a childless, retired widower, Frager suddenly found himself exiled to his native land. He spent a week in New York but there was too much of everything there—people, buildings, noise, culture—and so he moved into a hotel in Boston, a city he thought of as both lively and provincial, cleaving to tradition yet seething with young people. He strolled around the Common, traipsed the Freedom Trail, read the real estate advertisements, and rented a car. He thought he might settle in one of Boston's less flashy suburbs. The joke in the trade, one real estate agent confided, was that buyers should drive west until they could afford the mortgage.

The place Frager chose to live wasn't all that far west, close enough to the city to have both townies and commuters. Frager, being neither, briefly entertained a fantasy of joining the Unitarian church and participating in town meetings. If he felt isolated, it wasn't the town's fault. In fact, the place suited him well enough, and his new house, the first he'd ever owned, gave him both the odd thrill of owning property and something to do.

He puttered around the two-bedroom Cape with the gray clapboards and green shutters. His spurts of domestic activity were purposive, even necessary, but somehow felt like improvisations. His wife had been the clever shopper; Frager wilted after half an hour. So, he bought his new furniture at one store in one day. He found a place that sold kitchen gadgets, curtains and linens. One hour went to hanging his pictures and installing LED bulbs. Hedges surrounded the front yard, so he went to the hardware store and picked out a hedge trimmer and, as there was grass, a lawnmower as well. They had a garden store jutting into the parking lot. He took a cart and in ten minutes filled it with hosta, spirea, hibiscus, daylilies, then, on the way to the cashier, dropped in a bag of daffodil bulbs. He had to go back inside for a shovel.

The real estate agent who sold him the place was what his wife would have called soignée. She had expensive hair and drove a new black Audi. She had shown him several other properties in his price range, places with more space, more interesting or eccentric floorplans, more land.

"I'm curious," she said when the deal was struck. "Why'd you choose this house?"

Frager said, "Because it looks like you could just hose it out."

The agent handed over cards for a home inspector, an insurance agent, the local bank. He signed the purchase and sale agreement without haggling. She advised against a balloon mortgage.

"Okay, then. That's it. Get the inspection done. I'll see you at the closing."

Frager needed a project, a mental one, and thought he would like to write a scholarly article. He hadn't written anything of that sort since graduate school. That was when one of his professors, impressed by the ease with which he picked up languages, asked about his career goals. When Frager said he wasn't sure, the professor suggested he look into the foreign service. So, he had never felt a vocation; his career was in this sense accidental, faute de mieux. He took the exam, passed the security check, and was hired. It turned out that he liked the work and the travel too, at least before his wife got cancer.

Write what you know. The article would be about diplomacy. He had been a consul or deputy consul in lots of places and kept learning languages. But writing didn't come as easily as Turkish or Uzbek.

One morning, determined to get something down, he made coffee, gritted his teeth, and sat down at the computer.

Nothing came. Nada, zilch, rien. Then, with a smile, he typed, *Jewish husbands make the best slaves.*

When he came home from school on Wednesdays, his mother was usually playing mah jongg with three of her girlfriends. They'd grown up together, called themselves the Tootsies, had no secrets, and talked non-stop as the tiles clacked. Three dot. Two bamboo. They were of a generation and a class that seldom moved away or made careers and the longer they played and gossiped, the younger these women grew. Sometimes, Frager felt older than they were.

One Wednesday, as he came through the door, he heard his mother say, "Of course, Jewish husbands make the best slaves." This remark was greeted with girlish laughter.

A month or two later, he and his mother were shopping in Sears. She was looking for something in the stationery department where a dozen brands of typewriters were on display, each with a piece of paper on the platen. Frager typed *Jewish husbands make the best slaves* on every one then showed his mother.

She pretended to be furious, denied ever saying such a thing. It was hilarious. He went on teasing her about the sentence until it became a private joke between them.

Though Frager couldn't write he went on typing.

Slaves make the best Jewish husbands.

Husbands, make the best Jewish slaves!

The summer after the end of tenth grade, Frager signed up for a typing class. It was the most useful course he took in high school. Mrs. Roth was the Platonic idea of an office manager, champion and paragon of an insurance company's typing pool. Always professionally dressed, strict and nonsense-free as a pin, she was a good teacher. In addition to typing, she offered sound office advice. For example, she told her pupils always to fold any sheet of paper they discarded before throwing it in the wastebasket. "It saves room," she explained. It became a lifelong habit for Frager.

Before applying to graduate school in International Relations, he'd looked up the word *diplomacy*. It derived from the Greek for something folded in two, originally a document that conferred some privilege, like a passport. This was in the days before envelopes. Diplomacy, double, diploma, duplicity.

The quick brown fox jumped over the lazy dogs.

Mrs. Roth made them type that sentence over and over. "It uses the whole alphabet," she explained with her usual economy. Frager made an error, typed it again, then went on:

Lazy brown fox, quick! The dogs jumped over.

Lazy dogs jumped quick over the brown fox.

No writing going on, only typing, only rearranging.

Now is the time for all good men.

The time is now, all good men.

Good men, now is the time for all.

The best slaves. Lazy dogs and brown foxes. Good men.

Frager, bored and frustrated, gave up. The grass was mown, the hedges trimmed, the plants watered. He decided on a different project for the afternoon, cooking. In the Consul General's cookbook, he found a recipe for chili. A big pot of Texas chili sounded good. There would be dinners for half a week.

The recipe called for ground chuck, red kidney beans, crushed tomatoes, tomato paste, chili powder, onions, garlic, parsley, oregano, basil, cumin, celery, sugar, salt, green pepper, Tabasco sauce, and a bottle of Lone Star beer —"the indispensable ingredient".

On the way to the supermarket, he decided to make some changes: a hot pepper instead of a green one, cayenne pepper instead of Tabasco sauce, no stringy celery. He had no beer, no alcohol in the house at all.

Over dinner one night, his father said that one of their neighbors' marriage was on the rocks. His mother knew all about it. "Margie says he's taken to drinking alone," she had murmured portentously, "one of the first signs." The warning had stuck with Frager, like the folding of wastepaper. "Social drinking" was okay because the glass is a kind of prop, but never drink by yourself. He hadn't had so much as a glass of merlot or a dram of single malt since leaving the service and buying into a suburb.

Frager had an idea. He'd mess with Texas and pour in a bottle of stout instead of Lone Star which wouldn't be available in New England anyway.

Raleigh Liquors was on the corner of a strip mall next to Lucky Licks, the local ice cream parlor. Frager parked in the lot and started to the store. He was checking the cash in his wallet when he got to the door, so he was shocked when it flew open, just missing his face, and he collided with a man in a balaclava rushing out. He didn't see the man or the knife either. The knife went flying, so it didn't matter. The man crashed on top of Frager, swore, and tried to scramble to his feet, but their legs were tangled.

"Hold him!" yelled the young clerk.

Frager embraced the robber and held on while the clerk jumped on top of the both of them. The store manager, a woman who looked like she saw this sort of thing monthly, leaned casually in the doorway, coolly phoning the police on her cellphone.

There was an article in the local paper picked up by both a TV station and the *Globe*. The angle was ridiculous, something like *from mild-mannered diplomat to crime fighter*. Frager declined credit and to be photographed, but there were plenty of pictures of him on Google. The *Globe* chose one ten years out of date when he had more hair, fewer wrinkles, and brighter eyes. He was in his diplomat costume, so he looked like a consul rather than a habitué of liquor stores.

The consequences were good, though. The Guinness was on the house and the neighbors began to nod to him. He got a thumbs-up from local men driving by and a brace of women stopped by with admiring faces and tollhouse cookies.

That wasn't quite the end of it. There were also a pair of emails.

The chief business of a consul is business—promoting deals, making introductions, greasing the skids of profit. This was not Frager's favorite part of the job. He preferred the personal to the corporate and, while he regretted the messes his fellow citizens and local dissidents got into, he did enjoy getting them out of them when he could.

Somehow Sheila Romano found his email address—the official one was extinct, of course—but she did and wrote this:

Hi, Mr. Frager.

You probably won't remember me but I certainly remember you. I always will. Eight years ago, you got me out of jail in Izmir. I was backpacking that summer with my stupid, selfish pothead boyfriend. Jeff made me carry his stash because he said Muslim cops would never search a woman. You came to see me in that awful place, and you were so kind. Remember bringing me a pack of Oreos? A life-saver, like you. You contacted my parents and told me you'd do everything you could for me. And whatever everything was, it worked.

I saw an article about you catching a thief. It said you'd left the service and hinted that you'd been replaced. If the Administration did that, then it's just like Jeff. In fact, minus the weed, it is.

I'm married now, a registered nurse with two sweet boys. My husband's a Methodist minister (of all things) and we live in Oklahoma City.

I just wanted to thank you again and wish you all good things. As my husband would say, bless you.

The second email was from someone Frager remembered very well. It was written in Bulgarian.

My honored friend,

It has come to my attention that you have retired and caught a thief. The first is regrettable; the second is unusual. But you are an unusual man. A just man. After all, as a practical matter, justice means putting some people in jail and getting others out.

I am thinking that perhaps retiring was not your idea? Perhaps you disagreed with somebody who needed to be disagreed with? I know something about that.

Six years ago, in response to my exposé in the short-lived journal *Choveshki Prava*, I was tossed in a dungeon, interrogated, beaten, tortured, charged with sedition and the release of state secrets. An additional charge of embezzlement was added later, to show that my arrest was not political.

You made it your business to get me out, Mr. Frager. You didn't have to, but you crusaded for me. You made a public statement to the press and induced your Secretary of State to issue an official condemnation. Maybe all that was sufficient to secure my freedom, but I doubt it. On the one occasion that we met, you declined to tell me more but, however you managed my release, I am eternally in your debt.

I would like you to know that I now reside in Berlin where I continue my work on behalf of the rights of every single human being.

With gratitude and respect,

Vasil Chintalov

Frager had gotten Chintalov released by so far exceeding his brief that his career could easily have ended even earlier. He set up a private meeting with the Interior Minister to which he brought along a stick and a carrot. The former was the promise that all the Minister's assets in the United States would be frozen, the American banking system closed to him and the whole of his corrupt family. The carrot was the promise to find his youngest son a place in an American university. He actually did the latter. There was a certain admissions officer in Michigan, a poker player who in his Navy days had required some consular assistance.

Frager did two tours in Central America. A young American priest, inspired by the writings of Gustavo Gutiérrez, had come south to work with the indigenous farmers seeking land reform. He joined in field work, improved his accent, and delivered some rousing sermons.

While he was biking between villages, a car drove the priest off the road. Three masked men leapt out. None said a word as they delivered a ferocious beating. One of the attackers smashed the priest's bike with a tire iron, then his tibia. Nobody doubted that the attackers were disguised police.

Frager went to the hospital. The young priest's face was swollen. There were bandages around his torso; his right leg was in traction.

"They might have killed you," he said.

Though distorted, the priest's voice was firm. "Nearly did. We're all in God's hands, Mr. Frager, especially when doing His work."

"I can arrange for you to go home."

The priest groaned and shook his head. "No."

Frager sighed. He knew that those convinced of their own virtue are the most intransigent.

"What can I do for you?"

"Convince the government to help me in my work instead of arming the men who slaughter the poor."

Frager nodded, got to his feet, and said he'd be back.

During his second visit, Frager asked the priest if he knew about the Peasants Uprising in Germany.

"Of course. Luther condemned them."

"That's true. But he also inspired them."

Frager took out three folded papers and read from the first.

In Christendom all things are in common and each man's goods are the other's, and nothing is simply a man's own. The common man has long been brooding over the injury he has received in property, in body, and in soul. If I had ten bodies, I would most gladly give all to death in behalf of these poor men.

"Very fine words."

"Stirring ones. Luther's. When those words aroused the peasants and serfs, Luther wrote that he wanted to change people's relation to God, not to each other. Serfdom was fine with him, and he wrote a pamphlet condemning the peasants as robbers and murderers, calling for violence against them. When he published his notorious tract, the poor men replied with one of their own. They threw Luther's words back in his face and wrote with great dignity."

Frager unfolded the second sheet of paper and read.

Seeing that Christ has redeemed and bought us all with the precious shedding of his blood, the lowly as well as the great, we will retreat from our demands only if the social order is explained to us with arguments from Scripture. Otherwise we demand that each receive for his work according to the several necessities of all.

The priest smiled. "It's Marx before the fact."

"At Frankenhausen, the peasants had pitchforks and clubs. The overlords had cavalry and cannon. It was a massacre."

"The struggle is hard and long."

Frager leaned forward. "You want to be a martyr? Isn't that a temptation?"

The priest looked younger than ever; his swollen face shone.

"We have to attend to others, not ourselves. We have to give up any personal aggrandizement and share the pain of the others, the ones we care for. The good shepherd thinks first of his flock."

"And what if the shepherd leads the flock to a cliff?"

"Offering hope to the oppressed always leads to retaliation by those who profit from their despair. Isn't that what happened at Frankenhausen?"

"There are other ways."

"Have you suggested them to the government?"

"More than once."

"With what result?"

Frager was silent.

"The great sin of our time," said the priest as if giving a sermon, "is seeing oneself as the center of the universe."

"Where is the center?"

"Outside of us."

"God doesn't intervene."

"No. God is outside. He's waiting. You aren't a believer, are you?"

"No. Mostly not."

"Mostly?"

"Yes. I'm *that* kind of Jew."

"So, the God you don't believe in is the one who intervenes, the God of judgment? The omnipotent one? God is good before He is powerful."

Frager nodded and unfolded the third piece of paper. He read.

There is no quality and there is no power of man that was created to no purpose. Even base and corrupt qualities can be uplifted to serve God. To what end can the denial of God have been created? This too can be uplifted through deeds of charity. For if someone comes to you and asks your help, you shall not turn him off with pious words, saying, "Have faith and take your troubles to God!" You shall act as if there were no God, as if there were only one person in all the world who could help this man—only you."

"That was said long ago by Moshe Leib, a rabbi."

"And well said. Your rabbi understands. What's more, I think you do, too."

In that country at that time, American diplomats were afforded considerable deference. Frager had no trouble arranging a visit with the local Chief of Police, a man no less convinced of his virtue than the priest, and just as sure that he was a good Catholic.

The Chief sat behind a desk as substantial as he was. His uniform was clean and well pressed. The walls of his office were hung with framed photographs of him graduating, posing formally with his family, standing and smiling next to the President and the Bishop. There were pre-Columbian antiquities on the credenza and a bookcase with few books. He was large without being fat, had an intelligent face, and was about fifty. The Chief exuded confidence and a kind of refined brutality.

Frager was shown in and announced by a lieutenant.

The Chief stood and held out his hand. Skipping the niceties, he spoke at once. It was disarming.

“You’re here about your countryman, that naïve priest so deplorably attacked on the road.”

Frager took the offered hand. “I am,” he said.

“I assure you, Mr. Frager, we are investigating. It is a most regrettable incident.”

“Then I ask you to guarantee his safety. I visited him in the hospital. There were no guards.”

The Chief motioned for Frager to take a seat then sat himself.

“Who can offer such guarantees, especially in the current state of unrest? The hospital is safe, and I have no men to spare.”

Frager was silent for a few seconds.

“I’ve heard that you attend Mass every morning.”

The Chief pretended to be pleasantly surprised. “You’re well informed.”

“The church is dedicated to Saint Augustine, I believe.”

“Yes. The great Father of the Church.”

“You’ve read him?”

“My Jesuit teachers made sure of it. Augustine understood many things. He said it is our moral duty to respect the right to property and to obey the law.”

“Only the *just* laws.”

“Mr. Frager, our country has no unjust laws, though there are many who desire lawlessness.”

“And what if the property is stolen?”

“As to land, in this country it must be lawfully registered. In those rare instances when we discover it is not, we act.”

Frager paused again.

"You don't approve of what my young countryman is doing?"

"No, I do not, sir. And neither should you. Your young priest is a zealot for Karl Marx, not Jesus Christ. In my opinion, he ought to be re-educated or defrocked."

The Chief leaned back, enjoying the discussion. He pointed to the photograph of himself with the bishop, both of them in uniform.

"I am no less a shepherd than our good Bishop Gonzalez. I'm sure you've observed that our people are childish and have to be kept in order for their own benefit. They must be shown their duty to obey the law, including the laws regarding property. God is the supreme property owner, and it is our job to see that God's property is well tended."

"By those who own it lawfully?"

Here it was the Chief who paused.

"Mr. Frager, because people are endowed with free will but also with selfishness, the natural condition of humanity is not justice but injustice. Injustice is disorder. Our country is not like yours, not yet so orderly. I agree that certain of our actions are less than desirable, even sometimes a necessary evil. But in a state of disorder and rebellion what is necessary is good."

"It's not always easy to say what evil is necessary or how much."

The Chief folded his hands and smiled, relishing a game in which he had the upper hand. He probably had few such conversations.

"You mentioned Augustine," said the Chief. "The saint said that only God is perfect and all that God creates is good. Perfection cannot be corrupted, but what is merely good can be. The unfortunate truth is that people tend to lose part of their goodness, much of it, in fact. Evil is the absence of good but, even in the most depraved or misguided, you can still find some good. So, what needs to be done is to extirpate the evil. That is the way to cultivate the good—tear out the weeds and the grain can flourish. It is how I serve the state and God."

"They are the same?"

The Chief put his hands down flat on his desk.

"The Roman Empire was hardly a perfectly just organization; yet Augustine did not try to overthrow it. All sins are not crimes, but all crimes are sins. So, yes. I serve God by serving the State. Surely, Mr. Frager, somebody in your position, somebody who represents his government, must know that."

Frager paid one last visit to the hospital.

The young priest was feeling better and said he would be released at the end of the next week.

"You'll go back to what you were doing?"

"Certainly. It's how I serve God."

"That's a consolation? That you're serving God?"

"The greatest."

"I'm glad for you. But don't you think that consolation can sometimes be a hindrance?"

"How?"

"Have you read Simone Weil?"

"A woman to put us all to shame."

"Didn't she deny herself the consolation of baptism?"

"Yes, but she believed. She was a Catholic outside the Church. It's noble."

"What?"

"That she'd say she didn't want to cut herself off from non-believers."

"Ah. But didn't she turn her back on her fellow Jews, her forebears?"

"Not really."

"Not even the non-believing ones, like me?"

The young man smiled which made him look about sixteen years old. "You've reminded me of something else she wrote."

He paused.

"What was it?"

"Sorry. I was trying to recall the exact words. It's a hard saying—harder for me than for you, I think."

Frager waited, looking at the jacaranda outside the window.

"I think it went like this. Of two men who have no experience of God, the one who denies him is nearer to him than the other."

"I know of a rabbi who might agree," said Frager and smiled at the doomed young man who claimed to be consoled.

Shortly after, Frager was told he would be reassigned and granted a month's leave. He took it in the south of France and registered at his old pension in Nice, the Verdun. It was on the beach at Nice that he had met the perfect, adventurous Jeanne, as doomed by a mutated gene as the priest was by his faith. They had honeymooned there as well.

Frager picked up his customary copy of *Le Monde* on the way to the café where he was known. He was brought his brioche and coffee without needing to order. He sat in his usual spot and opened the paper. On page two he learned that the mutilated body found on a mountain road in South America had been identified as that of a young American priest. In empty, flowery language, the government expressed its official regret. The Chief of Police was quoted as saying that an investigation was underway.

Frager's article never took proper shape. What he wrote was rather a series of digressions, not very scholarly ones either.

He began with Benjamin Franklin. Franklin, he thought, was not only America's first ambassador but the most significant. But, instead of Franklin's diplomacy, Frager found himself writing about his headgear.

When Congress appointed him Minister to the French Court, Franklin sailed to Nantes and was wined and dined everywhere along the 150-mile route to Paris. Frager found that, according to a Frenchman of the time, everybody had "an engraving of Monsieur Franklin over the mantelpiece." When he joined Franklin in Paris, Adams groused jealously. "Franklin's reputation is greater than that of Newton, Frederick the Great or Voltaire, his character more revered than them all." But for that popularity, Frager mused, there might have been no Comtes de Rochambeau and Grasse besieging Yorktown and blocking the British fleet on Chesapeake Bay. And what was the source of Franklin's cachet with the French? Wanting to write of the historical abstract, Frager felt drawn to the quirky particular.

When he arrived in the capital, Franklin sported a small fur cap on his bald head. To the gathered crowd, evidently readers of Rousseau, America was à la mode and the fur cap proved Franklin was a rugged frontiersman with all the virtues of Jean Jacques' splendid savage. Never mind that he had won the Copley Medal, founded the University of Pennsylvania and most of the rest of the civic institutions of Philadelphia, wrote and published *Poor Richard's Almanac*; never mind the sophisticated wit, the inventions; never mind the kite and key.

What Frager admired in Franklin, what he believed made him an exceptional diplomat, was his understanding of human nature. Another man with such accomplishments might have indignantly corrected the silly assessment of the French. "A noble savage? *Moi*?" But Franklin made use of it. He sent home for a large supply of fur caps and made sure to wear one everywhere he went.

Thinking about the fur cap led Frager to recall a favorite story about Franklin. He had read it long ago in a book about practical jokes given to him as a graduation present by his freshman roommate, who had been exasperatingly fond of playing practical jokes. The gift itself was a practical joke.

Traveling on horseback through New England in winter weather, Franklin arrived at a tavern in the evening, half-frozen, starving, and wet. After having his horse stabled, he hurried into the tavern where he found all the seats near the fire filled with locals. He stood about shivering and dripping but no one made a place for him. He called for the landlord. "Do you have any oysters?" The landlord said that he did. "Good," said Franklin. "I want you to serve half a bushel of them to my horse." This attracted general attention. The landlord argued, but Franklin insisted. When the landlord started toward the stable with the pail of oysters, all the layabouts got up and followed. They'd never seen a horse that ate oysters. When they came back, Franklin had made himself comfortable in the best seat by the hearth. "Your horse won't eat the oysters," complained the landlord. "In that case," said Franklin serenely, bring them here and roast them on the fire. They'll do very well for my supper."

There they are, thought Frager, all the talents of the diplomat: thinking ahead, knowing what motivates those who frustrate you, deception, manipulation, self-interest. American independence was the seat by the hearth; the displaced loafers were le Roi's bankrupt treasury.

Thinking about the country's first ambassador led Frager to look into the country's first consul. This turned out to be James Maury, Jr, appointed American consul in Liverpool by George Washington. Suspecting things worked then as they do now, it was no surprise that

Maury had been a classmate of Thomas Jefferson who got Washington to appoint him. Liverpool was an important port and Maury was already doing business there. A lot of American businesses in Liverpool wanted their way smoothed and there was no dearth of American sailors getting into scrapes. Maury must have done his job well. He held it for thirty-nine years.

Frager figured Maury must have died at his post, but this was not the case. Andrew Jackson replaced him. Given his own situation, this interested Frager. The record didn't say why Maury was fired, but he could speculate. Jackson handed out lots of appointments to supporters; he not only invented the Spoils System, he publicly defended it. Then too, Maury was eighty-three years old. Frager found a letter Maury wrote to his son on the occasion of his stepping down. The discarded consul's words were dignified, any resentment buried under dutiful stoicism:

I have treated Mr. Ogden, I hope, with that respect due from a Consul of the United States to his successor. As to myself, I do feel rather out of joint, and I suppose I am to feel so for a time, but such things wear off and probably it will be so with me.

As it turned out, Francis B. Ogden did the United States a signal service. He befriended the inventor John Ericsson, who named his first screw-propeller steamboat the *Francis B. Ogden.* When the Royal Navy rejected Ericsson's designs, Ogden persuaded him to move to America and arranged financial backing for him. Ericsson is famous as the builder of the *U.S.S. Monitor*, the savior of the U.S. Navy at Hampton Roads.

As with Maury and Jefferson, a student friendship was behind Franklin Pierce's appointment of Nathaniel Hawthorne to the Liverpool post. The author despised the job yet performed it well. Frager looked into Hawthorne's journal and found that being consul in Liverpool offended his fastidiousness. American sailors he describes as "dirty, desperate, and all together pirate-like." He loathed visiting prisons, hospitals, asylums, inquests, and courtrooms. He seems to have been repelled by those he assisted, "all manner of simpletons and unfortunates." Almost the worst of all, he confided to his journal, were the Englishmen pretending to be Yankees. As a diplomat, it seems the upright Hawthorne was more often a victim of duplicity than a practitioner.

Diplomats have always been ethically suspect, even to themselves. The Jacobean politician Sir Henry Wotton, an ambassador, had the first famous one-liner on the matter: "An ambassador is an honest man sent to lie abroad for the good of his country." In his desultory reading, Frager had come across a couplet about what "being diplomatic" means to most people. It was composed by the writer and translator Isaac Goldberg, another deracinated Jew:

Diplomacy is to do and say

The nastiest things in the nicest way.

Tact and lying, lying tactfully. A folded paper.

Frager was thirty years younger than James Maury, Jr. was when he began his forced retirement. He would have liked to know what the old man did during his last nine years.

Frager knew he had to find something to do, something more than not writing articles and mowing the lawn. Retirement didn't suit him; it might even kill him. It was absurd. He lived alone in a neighborhood of families. He was a phony hero, certainly no scholar. He was not fitted to become a teacher, even if he could find a job.

Is there a sadder line in *Othello*, he thought, than the Moor's lament, *Othello's occupation's gone!*

Two years earlier, Frager had attended a weekend conference in Brussels. At the closing banquet, he had been seated next to a member of the Swedish delegation. They chatted pleasantly about the conference, transatlantic politics, the weather. But, when the coffee came, the woman turned to him almost aggressively.

"They tell me that you're a widower, and that you loved your wife dearly. I'm sorry."

Frager recoiled. "Thanks," he mumbled. "It's all right."

She persisted. "Is it? Is it really? Have you given up on women then, on sex?"

Frager's reply was brief, blunt, undiplomatic, a message not folded, and a revelation to himself. "Not women," he said almost brutally. "Intimacy." Then he excused himself and made his way back to his empty hotel room.

Dying Amandato

Beginning the big downtown rally at 4:30 was my idea. Bergstrom wanted it to start at noon, but I argued that would be a disaster. Pathetic crowds out on the streets, people heading to restaurants. Make it 4:30, I said. At that hour people would be leaving work, and just the sort we were after too. Even if they didn't know our candidate from a cheeseburger, which is what the polls suggested, we'd be sure of a crowd—maybe even a traffic jam. The news cameras would pick it up; the candidate might get charged up. Our own workers could scatter over the street carrying signs. I suggested they be handmade, to imply sincerity. By then I was giving the orders. I said that our guys would have to dress in business suits, silk blouses, good skirts. No jeans or T-shirts or running shoes. We wanted them to fit in, inspire confidence, a bourgeois upsurge. The whole point, I said, was to start a bandwagon. Bergstrom frowned all through my speech and his pale face turned shrimp-cocktail pink. I wound up delivering half a dozen commands and then I just walked out. I had some pressing business of my own, a toothache. The night before an old filling had popped out, one I'd had from childhood. Time was catching up with me. When I phoned my dentist's receptionist said she could maybe squeeze me at 2:15. I dug the drill. Dentists are always maybe squeezing you in whether they're busy or not. Right. Who wants a dentist with time instead of saliva on his hands? Sure enough, the waiting room was empty when I got there at 2:10 and it was just as empty when I left twenty minutes later.

I was coming out of the Medical Arts Building with that kind of invulnerable feeling you get after a bout of brief and useful pain when I ran smack into Schwager. He recognized me right off. I had no idea who he was, even after he told me his name. Maybe if I'd thought a minute or two, but I was contemplating the afternoon rally, Bergstrom's discomfiture, and my molar.

"Schwager. *Fred* Schwager," he said impatiently.

I shook his clammy little hand and smiled. I had shaken so many hands in the last two months that I might as well have been running for something myself. My grip was good and firm.

"We were at *college* together," he reminded me, as if apologizing for my poor memory. He made a show of being embarrassed on my behalf which in my experience is just a way people have of getting the upper hand when they've obviously got the lower one. Schwager wasn't being ironic, though; in fact, I don't think he's capable of anything so subtle as insincerity. No, he was glad to see me all right. The odd note was the anxiety to be off I could see in his face. If he was in such a rush, why stop me? I waited for him to excuse himself, but he didn't budge.

"Ah, *Schwager*, of course I remember you. Just wasn't expecting to see you is all." I clapped him on the shoulder as though we were at a class reunion in some ballroom and pointed at my mouth. "Just had a damned filling. Still hurts."

My fibbing heartiness seemed not to impress him. He shrugged off my hand. Clearly, Schwager wasn't the sort who shows up at class reunions; not successful enough. So, I kept waiting for him to buzz off and go wherever it was he was obviously in a hurry to get to but still he stayed in front of me, hesitating and actually blocking my way. Normally, of course, I'd have punched out quick, but I was in no particular hurry. It was fine with me to think of Bergstrom stewing back at headquarters and it was still a good two hours until the rally. My mouth hurt a bit, there was no major stuff to do at the office. I was at liberty.

So I asked him, "What're you up to these days?"

"Just like when I saw you last," Schwager replied, disappointed by the question. "Still at the bookstore, a little tutoring on the side. Same old thing. Things."

I remembered. I had run into him three or four years before at this seedy used bookstore he managed near the University. But there was more. Though it was not a recollection I cherished, Schwager and I had once been nearly close. This was during our sophomore year, and it lasted about a couple of weeks before I dropped him. Schwager had been what we used to call *intense*. Now he looked exactly like what he was bound to become: a balding bachelor eking out a living in the shadow of the university he'd never had the gumption to leave, every inch the forlorn intellectual, a professor manqué in a loose grey sweatshirt, wrinkled chinos, old-fashioned overcoat, granny glasses. Schwager had become one of those desperate clerks in the Russian novels he used to foist on everybody he met.

Schwager persisted in acting as if I were holding him up when it was the other way around. His unlined face seemed more innocent than wise, and I couldn't help wondering if he were still capable of the mental passions that had so impressed me for a few days when I was nineteen and wet as a puppy in a rainstorm.

Schwager was having an idea. You could see it taking shape. It was the same in the old days; you could always tell when he was having one. I remembered somebody joking about it; he compared the strain and sudden release to someone suffering with, then mastering constipation. He was screwing up his face the same way now.

"Look," he said, shuffling his feet and touching my arm, "you free?"

"In the chronological or existential sense?" This was an intellectual joke Bergstrom would never have gotten. I thought it apropos for Schwager.

Maybe he didn't get it either. He didn't laugh, he didn't even grin. He only hopped from one foot to the other. "Look, you remember Professor Amandato?"

"Amandato? Oh, yeah. Didn't we ? . . . God, when was it?"

Pleased, Schwager nodded and answered with animation. "When we were sophomores. I'm a little surprised you remember him."

"Oh, Amandato was a spellbinder, wasn't he? Hard to forget. But there's another reason I remember him. He gave me a C- when I ought to've gotten a B. You don't forget those things so easily, I guess. I'll bet *you* got an A, didn't you?"

He smiled, made wistful by the recollection of his ancient triumphs.

"So what about him?"

"Amandato's dying. I heard about it just a couple days ago. I've got this errand," he lied, "and I thought I'd go see him. Then I suddenly run into you. I mean we took his course together." Schwager paused a moment. "What I'm trying to say is it'd be easier for me if you'd come along. Classmates, you know. It might please him."

"What's he got?"

Schwager shrugged. "A case of death. What's it matter?" His nonchalance was transparent, but I checked my watch.

"It's just down to University Hospital. Only a ten-minute walk. Come on, what d'you say?"

I started to button up my coat. I pictured Amandato dying, propped up, my saying goodbye to him. The old mentor, a touching scene. "What the hell. Okay." I still had nearly two hours to kill anyway. I could play my part. Why not? I was pretty much over the C-. I could play bygones with a goner.

The instant I agreed Schwager relaxed, and in his gratitude he grew confidential. We headed down Chestnut Street past the fashionable leather shops, travel agencies, and banks, then over the river. By the time we reached the delicatessens, drug stories, and diners near the hospital he had become almost familiar, as if our archaic and momentary friendship had never been cut off at all. In fact, I was astonished by how large a few weeks of our sophomore year seemed to have loomed in his life.

"You know, Amandato's class really changed me," he said. "To tell you the truth, nothing existed for me that fall except his lectures—and you. Oh yes, it's true. I looked up to you, not the same way I did the Amandato, of course. You were my own age of course and, in that sense, I guess I saw you as a kind of model for myself. I quickly realized that I was wrong about that, that I had it just backwards."

This was not flattering but, on the other hand, it was silly. "How?" I asked, feeling not so much rejected as a role-model as superior because a time I could barely remember was still so vivid to him. For me one year of undergraduate life now seemed no different from the others; it was all a blur of dull lectures, feverish exams, bad coffee, cold dorms, drunken parties, interchangeable coeds, callow posing and nebulous ambitions. Schwager might as well have been talking about elementary school. Amandato's forgotten course, collegiate enthusiasms, dead friendships seemed to me to have nothing to do with what I now was. No doubt, I thought looking over at him, Schwager's development had been arrested, while I had achieved authentic maturity, a definite place in the real world. I could have been talking to a child, or rather the ghost of one.

"There was the night you threw up on my windowsill, four stories up, and ended by crying about some girl named Melissa. Remember? I think she stood you up or something."

"No. I don't remember any Melissa. *Or* throwing up."

"Naturally, I could never be like you," Schwager went on blithely and with a dismissive laugh. "I mean you were everything I wasn't, that was it. You were stylish, at ease in your skin, a sentimental materialist like all men of the world. You liked to *have* things. Know what I mean?"

I was not displeased. "Really? That's how I seemed to you?"

Schwager nodded. "That's why I broke off our friendship. It's too late now and sort of silly, but I want to apologize. I wanted to at the store that time but—"

I laughed. "*You* broke it off? Broke *what* off?"

Schwager slowed down and considered. "Well, *it* was broken off, let's say. Our friendship. No matter how or who, right?" He was trying to be generous, to spare my feelings. It was more than just insulting.

I had no wish to argue over something so absurd. The business about my crying over some girl annoyed me; he must have made it up. Well, I would let him keep his illusions, since he seemed to need them. So I dropped it. "What about the professor, then? Did he disappoint you too?"

Schwager picked up his pace and threw his arms around as he spoke of Amandato. The very idea of the man galvanized him.

"What can I say? I wanted to *be* Amandato. Really, I suppose that's what it amounted to. I put him on a pedestal. He was the source of light. But how can you *become* the light you see by? No, he didn't disappoint me. I just wanted too much. In a way, my friendship with you was tied up with it. You see, it was Amandato I admired. I used you, I think, to fight against that attraction, to resist something I was drawn to but believed beyond my powers. Amandato *was* something. It wasn't what he *had* but what he was. Oh, never mind. It's hard to explain."

I answered mockingly. "So while I *had* things, he *was* something? So I was—what? Darkness to his light? Is that it? Having to his being?"

Then, to my astonishment, Schwager said something quite solemnly. "To me you were the world."

"What? The whole world?"

"World*ly*. You were fraternities and split-level houses and three-piece suits and, in due course, the University Club."

I laughed. People like Schwager always consider people like me shallow. It's their consolation.

"I'll bet you eat there at least once a week," he said.

"Oh, at least twice!" I felt like rubbing it in.

"Exactly."

"So why didn't you go to grad school and become Amandato?"

We were now outside the hospital and so Schwager let himself off the hook. "I'd rather not talk about it. Not now. I think we go in here."

We went to the information desk and asked for Amandato's room number. In a whisper Schwager begged me to do it. Even that was too much for him. The holy-of-holies and all that.

"Amandato—what a lot of visitors *he* gets," said the woman, pulling a card and raising a pair of hideous glasses that hung around her neck. "You're in luck. Looks like they're letting people in today. It's Room 515." She dropped her glasses, leaned forward, and pointed. "The elevators are that way."

Hospitals are like ships. Everything is whitewashed and smells peculiar. Floors are forever being swabbed. The lordly doctors stroll their rounds like commodores and admirals; the orderlies and nurses who actually run things listen to their commands resentfully. Guests have to be given permission to come aboard, to march up the gangplank into this machine-choked world where everything is man-made and functional and repellent. All the passengers are sick, sailing on a grey sea, hoping to make it to port. Linoleum and stainless steel. Horrid green and white walls.

The door of Amandato's room was half open. Schwager hung back so I went in first. Room 515 was semi-private but held only one patient. The Professor's bed had been cranked up at a sharp angle so that he was nearly upright and only five feet away from me. He looked much the same. I recognized the old ferocity and the derisive cut to his thin-lipped mouth; there was the narrow head topped by a tuft of hair that made him look a little like an asparagus. The hair was grey now and the mouth tighter, but otherwise he had altered rather little, even though he was dying. In the corner by the window sat a fat old woman with hair dyed black and a plaid shawl over her shoulders. Her whole face was pursed and sour. A big box of chocolates lay in her lap. A jungle of flowers and plants appeared to be growing out of the radiator to her left. At the foot of the Professor's bed, only the length of a baseball bat in front of me, a woman of about twenty-five clad in an over-sized chamois shirt, leather trousers, and high boots was adjusting a video camera. Seated on the empty bed was another woman. She was wearing a dark crimson skirt with a clashing purple sweater and examining a small piece of yellow paper. She glanced up at me as I crossed the threshold.

"And who're you?"

The challenge took me aback. Schwager, suddenly assertive, squeezed through the door and leapt into the breach.

"Former students of Professor Amandato," he declared rather heraldically, nodding meaningly at the Professor himself, who had shifted his eyes toward us without turning his head, like a bird of prey.

"God! All these damned people," muttered Ms. Leather.

"So?" said the other. "What do you want? You're not supposed to be here, you know."

She spoke as if she owned Amandato. As I saw it, Amandato was effectively on public display, already lying in state, so to speak.

"We're here to visit, obviously," Schwager said crossly.

The Leather Lady answered next, still playing with her machine. "We're here making a movie and we weren't supposed to be disturbed. You're obviously going to be in our way, so why don't you just run along and come back another time?"

"A movie?" Schwager sounded impressed.

"Documentary," she explained still not looking up from her camera. "I'm Keena—that's Philippa. Pictures here—text there."

Both Schwager and I, side by side now just inside the door, looked toward the old woman planted in the corner with her chocolates.

"I'm the wife," she croaked in an under-used voice, which was about as welcoming as her face. "So naturally I don't have any rights in the matter," she whined. The corner's just the place for her, I thought.

It was a day of surprises for Schwager. He gave a start and then said something truly stupid. "His wife? I always thought the Professor was a bachelor."

"Hmpf," sniffed the wife. "So did he, most of the time."

"Look, if you won't leave can you just do whatever you came for quickly?" begged the exasperated Keena. "The light's particularly good right now and who knows how long we've got?"

All three women glared at us. I turned to look at the Amandato who hadn't said anything and who still wasn't moving his head.

"Can he hear us?" I asked.

"Christ! Of *course* he can," said Philippa. She was, after all, about to become the cinematic expert on Amandato; she already was.

"How are you, Professor?" Schwager offered in his rather stupefied way, taking a step toward the bed and holding out his hand.

Amandato regarded him impassively. I think one hand might have twitched a little but that was it.

"Naturally, he can't *talk*," explained Keena. "Cancer of larynx does that, you know."

"We didn't," I said.

"You didn't know?"

"About the cancer. About the larynx."

Philippa held up the little piece of paper she'd been reading. "He writes notes. See? Conversation-slips I call them."

"When he *wants* to," added Keena dryly and Philippa laughed. It was an in-joke. Cancer of the larynx.

Mrs. Amandato opened up her box of chocolates, carefully selected one, and popped it in her mouth. "Umm," she said with satisfaction.

Schwager drew still nearer to the bed.

"Professor," he began. "Professor, I'm Frederick Schwager. I'm sure you don't remember me. I mean even if you did give me an A it was such a long time ago. Twenty years, actually. My term paper—"

"For God's sake," muttered Keena, who now had her camera all squared away and was hoisting it onto her shoulder. Philippa just giggled.

Schwager turned red and looked appealing toward me, just like a little boy teased by the girls.

"Look, Professor," I explained in the irresistible voice I had deployed to stunning effect earlier in the day, a voice equable, self-possessed, and deep, "Schwager here and I were both students of yours a couple decades ago. In fact, we were in the same class. We ran into each other by accident this afternoon. Schwager'd just heard about your illness and that you were here in University Hospital. He suggested we pay our respects. You see, you've meant a lot to us over the years.

What you taught us stuck. We owe you more than we can say. We came to tell you."

"Yes," chimed in the earnest Schwager. "You've been the lodestone of my life, Professor. It was because of you—"

Lodestone? And he thought *I* was sentimental?

The Professor raised his left hand, palm out, like a traffic cop. That stopped Schwager in mid-adoration. Then he rotated his hand sideways and fluttered his index and middle fingers as if calling for a cigarette. Philippa, who was still lounging on the empty bed, got to her feet and fetched a clipboard from the metal table between the beds. "He wants to write something," she explained, not without an air of disappointment.

She laid the clipboard on the professor's lap and handed over a black felt-tipped pen. A small yellow pad was affixed to the clipboard. Amandato wrote quickly and ripped off the top sheet. It was one of those pads with weak glue on one end for sticking on things. He motioned for me to come closer and then, with a surprisingly sudden movement, smacked his communiqué on my right sleeve.

"What's it say?" demanded Schwager eagerly, already reaching for it.

I lifted the note off my coat slowly, glanced at the sneering, impatient Keena, for whom one picture was worth a thousand words, and at Philippa, who looked as though whatever Amandato had written properly belonged to her. The Professor's handwriting is best described as undulating; however, it was legible enough. I read the note aloud: "*When was the Council of Nicaea?*"

Keena guffawed; the old lady stoked herself with another bon-bon; Philippa put her hands on her hips and swayed like a Spanish dancer. "Let me see that," said Schwager, as if I'd made it up. I handed over the note.

The Professor was already writing another. This one took a little longer.

"Third century?" Schwager guessed.

"No," said Philippa. "Fourth. 325 A.D, to be precise. Rejection of the Arian heresy. The Council adopted a creed founded on that of Eusebius of Caesarea. A little later, upon the conversion of Constantine, the Western World went all Christian."

Poor Schwager was annihilated.

Amandato stuck his new note on my sleeve. This time I did not read it aloud.

"*To examine a question,*" he had written, "*is to bare one's teeth, to bite it. Teaching is writing on water. Smoking was more rewarding than teaching the likes of you. Don't flatter me. It's despicable.*"

I handed the slip to Schwager, who staggered.

"According to the Professor," Philippa observed, reading a note from her own collection, "*The equality of death, a consolation in the hierarchical fourteenth century, is an affront in the democratic twentieth.*"

Schwager sounded like he was gasping for breath.

For some reason I felt like defending the poor bastard and demanded as brutally as I could, "Why exactly are you ghouls here?"

Keena stuck her tongue out at me and took a note from her breast pocket. "*I have all my life hated the books I loved. I often longed to rape coeds, particularly the ones in the second row.*"

"*I wore my light-weight learning as ponderously as possible,*" continued Philippa, responsively. "*After all, it was my armor.*" She crossed her arms and smiled triumphantly.

"Oh, I get it. So, the life of the mind's a fraud? Is that it? Well, big deal," I said. "There, I've hit on the theme of your little documentary, haven't I? You think this is news? Authority's mortal? Clay feet are connected to clay legs? Come on."

Schwager had plumped down on the end of Amandato's bed. Gradually he composed himself and now he made quite a little speech.

"Professor," he said with more dignity than you'd have expected, "you're obviously being hard on yourself. That's clear. You never once told us what to believe. You taught us that real authority depends entirely on faith, that there's no point in granting it to those who are always right, those who convince by force of argument or the weight of their evidence. Convince. Force. You told us that these are military metaphors. It's the one who's believed in the absence of evidence who has true authority. I remind you of it now. Believed even in spite of himself. And if that's true, Professor, then you can't despise your students. Not even the forgettable or the failed ones, like us. We were the source of your authority, Professor Amandato." Having said this, Schwager fell to cleaning his glasses on his sweatshirt.

"God! Did you get any of that down, Philly?" asked Keena, suddenly energized, moving her camera into position at the end of the bed.

The Professor began writing again, scrawling hurriedly, tearing off sheet after sheet. You could see that the effort was exhausting him, draining away his vitality, but he pressed on nonetheless. We could all see that he was shrieking on paper.

"You're killing him!" shouted the wife from her corner. She tried to haul herself out of her chair but only succeeded in sending the chocolates flying and knocking over a geranium. Keena swiveled professionally, one knee bent, to catch the action.

I reached for Amandato's notes and began reading them aloud even as he continued writing them.

"I can imagine another Socrates," he had begun. *"This one is guilty, guilty. Plato leaves out the prosecution's case, doesn't he? Plato's just another case of puppy love. Same with all disciples. We vampires live off their love. Teaching is the only form of social life we can manage. Power. We have to be in charge. But my Socrates despised his students. He seduced Alcibiades and hoodwinked Crito. We know his type, don't we? Xenophon did. . . .* "

"You've been killing him all his life," protested Mrs. Amandato, still stuck fast. "All of you. You made him nervous and he smoked and smoked." She kept struggling upward.

I went on. *"Xantippe, the old shrew, knew the truth, like all shrews."* I looked to the wife and resumed. *"What of Socrates's sons? He had sons, remember. Auto mechanics. Gamblers. Gluttons. Cowards. Jailbait. Socrates was a con man. Just when we use up the very last bit of our knowledge we stop, letting you all believe there's plenty more where that came from. Just a bag of tricks of which the subtlest is the protest that we know nothing at all. We hate what we say and who we say it to. Power, power. And yet . . .* "

The notes stopped.

Schwager rose and moved almost threateningly toward Keena and her camera.

"Give me those," commanded Philippa, leaning right across the Professor to get the slips of paper away from me. She actually clawed at me with her long hands.

"The spell is greater than the magician," swore Schwager, as if reciting a dogma. He let Keena alone and sat down again. I let Philippa have the conversation-slips which she began reading greedily.

The Professor wrote something quickly, shaking his head. I think he intended it for me, but Philippa tore the note from him before I could see it.

"Ha!" she exclaimed. "Listen to this. *There are no pleasures of the mind, only degrees of pain.*"

"As for me," I found myself saying angrily, "I chose the *real* world. The world where things really *happen.* Not artsy-fartsy home movies or the refuge of a bookstore. And definitely not the hothouse drama of some stuffy classroom."

The Professor turned to look at me. His eyes narrowed to a squint. His wife had finally struggled to her feet and was now waddling toward the bed. While everybody was in motion Amandato scribbled a short note, folded it, and pressed it right into my hand. His fingers were dry and terribly cold.

Keena hovered over him with her camera, as if it were a microscope. Mrs. Amandato, sniffling and wheezing, tried to insert herself into the frame. Philippa stood aside to make room for her.

"That's great! Hold it right there," hummed Keena, looking intently into her viewer.

"You all failed him," said the old woman bitterly, already in tears, already using the past tense. She laid her fat, spotted hand on her husband's narrow chest, as if she wanted to push him down into the bed.

But Amandato shoved her hand aside, drew himself away from the bed and sat up precariously. He looked around, at all of us around his deathbed, his eyes flashing and yet already beginning to dim. I suddenly noticed how dark the room had grown. As if he hadn't said enough already, Amandato seemed to want to make a last proclamation and grunted horribly through what might have been a sentence or two. Perhaps it was a condemnation; it could even have been love. There was no way to tell. Keena moved in tight. Mrs. Amandato cried out her husband's first name.

"This is it," hissed Philippa, sucking in her breath.

Schwager ran from the room yelling, "I'm going for a nurse!"

As if he had been shoved, Amandato collapsed across the bed, one arm striking the metal rail with a disgusting sound. His eyes rolled back in his head.

Philippa bent over as if to kiss him. "He's only fainted," she offered clinically.

"I'm getting it," said Keena, excited, running her camera like a lover's curious hand up his wasted torso all the way to his anguished yet blank face.

Turning away from this scene with distaste, I opened my note. It was only two words, a subject and a predicate. *You plagiarized.*

It was night when I finally got back to the office. Bergstrom wasn't there. Nobody was. The rally had been over for hours.

Ein Heldenleben

One Sunday morning at the end of July, just a week after my wife and I got back from our trip to France, Victor moved into the second-floor bathroom. Apart from his refusal to come out he seems to me not so much greatly changed as greatly changing. With me, at least, he is if anything more communicative than before. My wife insists otherwise. Now that she is unable to see him, to smother him with kisses and rearrange his hair, she worries that he has hit his head on the side of the tub, passed out from spitefully holding his breath, is lying on the tiles convulsed by some sort of seizure. It's true that he hardly has a word to say to her, but she forgets that for the last couple years he has had little to say to either of us. However, when she could look at his face and see that he was being sullen his silence troubled her less. "It's just a stage," she would say dismissively. I understand. After all, she was never a fourteen-year-old boy.

That first Sunday she pleaded with me to break down the door. My instinct was to leave the boy alone. I tried the best I could to reassure her, but she wouldn't give it up. Finally, just to satisfy her, I called in to the boy.

"All right, Victor, what would you do if I smashed in the door?"

"What do *you* think?" His voice was even and menacing.

These, his first words, the rhetorical question of a Socrates or a shrink, were nearly too much for his mother's morbid imagination but at least they stopped her nagging me.

"Look, he'll probably be out in an hour," I said.

Should I be surprised that my wife, so protective of Victor, should be eager to employ violence in this instance, or at least for me to use it?

If we ex-hunters hadn't forgotten everything we used to know, we'd tip-toe around mothers, especially the ones who can't see, feel, and smell their young whenever they want. Where Victor is concerned my wife is no different from a she-bear or lioness. The way she fussed over him used to worry me until I saw how the boy resisted. I was secretly pleased by the way he'd move his head aside or re-muss his hair. He never defied her openly, never made a scene or used a harsh word to his mother; he simply shrank away, recoiled like a sea polyp. I can see how his craving for inviolability might have turned into a motive. However, I haven't presumed to suggest reasons for Victor's change of domicile, not to my wife and especially not to Victor. I have the feeling that my claiming to understand him would wound him more than anything.

"Victor didn't run away," I remind my wife. "A lot of kids his age do, you know. Or they sniff things. Quite a few hang themselves."

"You're awful. It's the same as if he *did* run away," she retorts, displeased with me but nonetheless wanting me to go on unsuccessfully comforting her.

"I'd say *run* and *away* are the two things he didn't do. In fact, he just took a few steps further inside."

She looks me up and down. "You know what you are? You're just like that boulder, the one the Piatellis built their house on top of. You can hold a place up, but you don't *feel* anything."

Margot is naturally outraged that she has to share our bathroom. It's a real hardship for her but my wife finds it difficult to sympathize. "She could show a little more compassion for her brother," she says. In my opinion, this is not expecting too much of Margot, just the wrong thing. She's not at a particularly compassionate age on top of which she's never cared for her brother, not even the idea of him. Frankly, Margot despises Victor. Even to dislike a person requires some familiarity with him, some notion of his character and interests, not just his bad habits. But soon after Victor was born Margot took up toward him an attitude of studied indifference, as if he were literally not visible to her, had flown in under her radar. This has not helped her relationship with her mother, though my wife has always tried to be scrupulous about showing favoritism. I know how she worries about driving the girl away. I've often heard her pleading with Margot: "Just remember, you're the only two people in the world with the same blood running through your veins!" The desperation in this ritual appeal to blood sometimes amused and at others frightened me.

Margot's most intimate involvement with her brother came when he was two and she was six. She put pink polish on her brother's nails and pinned a pink bow in his hair. She was too young to think she was humiliating the boy, though not too young to want to turn him into her doll. It was the precursor of the teenage siren's urge to enthrall and enslave.

Over the last couple of years, when ignoring him has become impossible, Margot took to composing insults on little slips of paper and taping them to Victor's door. My wife showed me a few of these notes. I had to admit they were well written and inventive. My daughter has a real talent for invective.

Victor took some clothesline, a pulley, and the necessary hardware into the bathroom with him. He has no wish to starve. He laid his plans with care. I saw to it that he didn't even miss breakfast that first Sunday. My wife objected to my abetting him, sending him up whatever he wanted in a bucket. The neighbors would see. On the other hand, how could she deprive him? Poor dear, she just wasn't able to accept the situation. She believed it was only a matter for cajolery, bribes, or guilt, as if he weren't fourteen but nine. All of these she tried in rapid and, from Victor's point of view, predictable succession. He simply ignored her. In fact, I was the only one Victor would talk to that day and, at first, only on purely technical matters. His voice sounded distant and military, like radio messages from Mission Control.

I went to his door after he'd lowered the breakfast things. "Do you really think you can stay in there?" I asked him, not angrily, with an emphasis on the *really*, but out of sincere curiosity.

"It's July," he said, "I'm not missing any school."

"That's true, but what about September?"

There was a pause. "*Sufficient unto the day is the evil thereof.*"

I should explain. My wife's father was a Methodist minister, and this was his favorite Bible verse. He habitually cited it whenever anybody foolishly tried to share their worries with him. Victor must have heard it a dozen times when he was little and I suppose it stuck. The line always reminded me that my father-in-law lived in a furnished parsonage free of charge. At sixty-five he retired comfortably to Scottsdale. He did not quote this verse when he got the word about his colon cancer.

"Just tell me, Vic, what is it you want?"

"To be left alone and to be very, very small."

I admit it. I'm proud of my son. He charms me. When he wanted something to read, I asked what he'd like and he said, "Oh, just suppose you were me and felt like reading and then give me that."

He finished the long novel I chose for him in only three days and asked for another book "by the same guy." He didn't even try to pronounce Dostoyevsky. It was touching.

Victor's bathroom sits between his old room and Margot's rosy boudoir. Our bedroom, the "master," is at the other end of the house. Now if poor Margot wants to take a shower she has to go through our bedroom. For her other needs she has appropriated the powder room downstairs. Luckily, before he locked himself in Victor removed her paraphernalia, laid it all neatly outside the door, the bottles lined up like a little army, the tubes stacked neat as artillery shells.

One evening I peeked into the powder room after Margot had gone out with her friend Sheila. It was tiny to begin with, but she had crammed the room with an astonishing quantity of stuff: cosmetics, a blow dryer with a huge nozzle, curlers, jars of creams to cover pores and bottles of astringent to re-open them, colored pastes, conditioners and shampoos, tubes of sunblock, perfumes—the full panoply of nubility. Seeing all these things in such a small space made me despondent; I realized how little I knew my daughter and that I would only know her less and less. She was gone even before she left. How did this happen? In the usual way. Little by little Margot and I fell into a well-made play about mutual disenchantment. Just when we should have been talking to each other about weighty matters with complete honesty, like serious adults, nothing seemed less possible. I tried to remember the first time I came home from work and she didn't rush to meet me. I couldn't.

That night I had a dream that threw me for a loop. It was sexual, raw, unprecedented. I think I was in a huge bathroom in Paris, but the peripheral details are cloudy. In this dream I had oral intercourse with Margot's friend Sheila. Worse yet, it was a wet dream, the first in at least a decade. I awoke full of self-loathing, frightened, guilty, ashamed, perplexed, sticky. I thought almost at once of my son. Victor was fourteen; he was the one at the wet-dream age, not me. But for a moment I was fourteen too.

I crawled out of bed, went barefoot down the hall, and tapped at the door of Victor's tiled hermitage. I could see the light under the door. "It's me," I whispered.

"Go back to bed, Dad," he said. "Stavrogin's just bit the governor's ear."

There were more erotic dreams, not every night but about twice a week. Mostly I was able to wake myself before anything decisive happened. One night I shook myself into consciousness and discovered I had an erection that felt twice normal size. My member did not feel part of me but as if it had been extruded like some huge, throbbing hernia. I imagined a lust-maddened homunculus pushing as hard as he could. As usual I had been dreaming of a teenage girl—not Sheila this time, just some generic nymphet. These dreams were unbearably shameful. In agony but fearful of waking my wife I tiptoed down to Margot's powder room. When I opened the door a thick wave of toilet water, face power, and hair spray—all sorts of feminine fragrances—hit me and my senses swam. I had to step outside to clear my head. I took a deep breath before diving back in. I quickly doffed the bottom of my pajamas, found a washcloth, soaked it in cold water and pressed it around my overheated, swollen member as one might tweeze a surfeited tick.

Victor asked me for a *Playboy* and any book by "Ballazack".

"The magazine I understand, but why Balzac?"

He replied in a don't-you-know-anything tone. "That other guy, the Russian," he still hesitated with the uncertainty of the auto-didact, "Dustyoffsky, he learned to write novels by translating Ballazack."

So, Victor had been reading the introductions as well.

"And I'd like a deck of cards and a box of Hershey bars, please. And a couple of batteries for my Walkman."

"Hershey bars and batteries, okay, but no *Playboy*."

"Why not?"

"Because I get to decide."

Silence.

"Tell me, how are you sleeping? Okay?"

"I sleep fine."

"No, I mean *where*. In the tub?"

"Where else am I going to sleep?"

"You don't lie down in the water?"

"Sure, when it's hot."

I was troubled by an image of his face—it was getting hard to remember it—sinking beneath the cooling water. My heart ached. "Don't you miss your friends? Don't you miss television, Nintendo, riding your skateboard, smelling the grass?" I was sure he didn't; I only said it to drive away the mental picture of an inundated, completely indifferent face.

There was a pause while he let the stupidity of my questions dissipate. "I don't know about you, Dad, but solitude's something I handle best when I'm alone."

Isn't that a kick? Isn't that really something? Solitude's best handled when alone. A stab at Dostoyevsky? A puerile contradiction? Not to me who always has to be dragged to dinner parties. "See? You were the life of the party," my wife would say as we drove home, and I vowed never again. I would have liked to tell her that was the worst of it, actually, that I really am the life of a party, that I joke and smile; but even I didn't have a clue as to why I always felt fouled by my good cheer. Now my son had wrapped it up for me in a single *bon mot.*

I've come to cherish many things Victor says for their purity. He's made me aware that I'm surrounded by people who speak in clichés, who make them up on the spot. For instance, I was listening to one of Margot's friends the other day. "Well," she said, "it doesn't get *my* elevator to the penthouse." It's like living on television.

Margot leaves for college on Labor Day. It's obvious she can hardly wait. Who can blame her?

"Do you think he'll come out once she's gone?" my wife asks with guilty hopefulness.

Her question makes me glum. I realize how unhappy she's become, how resigned, and that I'm responsible. I wanted to cheer her up and idiotically made a joke about our trip to France. "Well," I said twitching my lip, "at least we'll always have Paris."

She burst into tears. "If only we hadn't gone!"

I bought two copies of *Père Goriot*. I thought Victor and I could talk about the book together, but he gave it up after only a few chapters.

"It's boring," he said. "How about some more Russians?"

"Why Russians?"

"I don't know. I guess I just like them. It's like, I don't know, like Dustyoffsky reads me when I read him."

The next day I bought him a copy of *Notes from Underground*. I found my old Dell paperback from college. The pages were yellow and brittle.

Margot delivered a speech over dinner, or instead of it. The strange thing is she never raised her voice. She was a great bawler in her infancy and quite a histrionic whiner thereafter. Perhaps this frigid self-possession is another sign of how little remains of the daughter I knew. It was shattering to hear this reasonable, equable, knowing, relentlessly judgmental voice riddling us with .45 caliber adjectives. Margot probably was making a great deal of sense but what she said kept going out of focus. After the first couple of minutes, I heard only the over- and undertones. The speech lulled me. I suppose I withdrew into an irresistible weariness. I tried to stifle a yawn and failed. Margot stopped in mid-sentence, gaped at my gaping mug, stood up and threw her plate against the wall. Then she ran upstairs. Illogically, I wondered if she had decided to join her brother.

"I could kill you," said my wife metaphorically. I looked at this stressed-out, semi-abandoned, pitiable, middle-aged woman sitting at the table she had picked out with such care, with so much hope at Rothman's twenty years before, no doubt imagining the buoyant dinner parties she would give for convivial, witty guests. I had an impulse to put my arm around her and hold her as tight as if she were the whole of priceless, precarious civilization. I wanted to tell her things were certainly in flux but that everything would be all right. The impulse passed. I was too deflated, too helpless. I felt like yawning again. I decided to hide behind male clumsiness.

"I guess you should go up to her."

"Why not go *together* for a change? Do you think you could manage to stay awake?"

"She might feel outnumbered."

"God."

"All right, but you do the talking, okay? I don't want to say anything that'll make things worse."

As we trudged up the stairs my wife was already trying to reassure herself. "Margot's at a very vulnerable stage right now. She's about to leave home. It's separation anxiety. And, of course, her little brother's in the bathroom."

"*Her* bathroom," I mumbled.

Margot wouldn't let me in. She and her mother talked for over an hour with the door shut. Whenever I hear female laughter I'm sure it's directed at me.

Victor has discovered negative self-definition. "I don't know what I want to be, only what I don't."

What he chiefly doesn't want to be, of course, is me. On this point I understand him perfectly; but I can't bring myself to tell him that I feel the same, that the True Way has just eluded me for three decades longer than it has him, and that you only think it's stopped eluding you if you give up looking for it. I don't want him to hear such things from me. I don't want to hear myself saying them.

When I was Victor's age, I was still going to the summer camp my parents sent me to in Vermont. For eight weeks each summer I lived the life of a healthy animal. It was all sports, good fellowship, joyous competition, baseball, tennis, swimming, canoe trips. We read comic books and adventure novels and talked ignorantly about sex and war. There were things written on the dark wooden walls of the bunks (I can still conjure up the smell of heated pine boards), messages fingered on in toothpaste going back to the 30s and the 40s. One in particular sticks in my mind. "Bunk V — V jerked on V-J Day." The camp had not survived the 60s. Anyway, I don't think Victor would have liked it there. Even I, in my last year, had felt ill at ease. What had always been so natural had become unbearably artificial.

My wife began to ask me a rhetorical question but halfway through it turned serious. "Don't you *want* him to come out?" You could see it in her face, the moment when it occurred to her that maybe I really didn't want her baby to come out. She looked at me like an enemy. "Of course I want him to come out, only I don't want to force him." Everything's crumbling, I thought, everything soft. Is there anything around here that *isn't* soft?

She must have seen something in my face too, something that drove her back from the brink. She cocked her head and examined me. "What's the matter with you?" she asked so gently that for a moment I thought she was going to reach for my forehead, the way she used to do with the children. A beautiful maternal gesture, the hand slightly cupped.

Victor's not soft. He wants to be small the way a pebble is small, to become gritty and irreducible as a bit of gravel. Yet his mind is malleable and it's growing so fast and fiercely you can almost hear it.

Last Saturday I stood at the kitchen sink eating a piece of watermelon, spitting the seeds straight into the disposal. I could see into the yard next door. The Hoffmans' daughter and granddaughter were visiting for the weekend. Julia was hanging out some sheets while her little girl, no more than four, skipped around the yard. I found myself examining the child closely. She kept her eyes on the ground as though looking for money or worms or four-leaf clovers. When she tired of skipping, she ran over to one of the poles from which the clothesline was strung. She grasped the pole with her arm fully extended, placed her feet close together at the base and began to rotate around and around. I could see her mouth moving. She was singing. Her eyes were on her sneakers. They looked new. Maybe she became dizzy because she suddenly stopped, fell on her back, and looked straight up into the sky.

I was fascinated. No adult could do this, could move that way, could feel so close to the earth and the clouds. For her everything happened completely in the present; life was weather without forecasts.

My talks with Victor made me fall into nostalgia, remembering how I too had been bitten by Raskolnikov, deep enough so that when I got to college I wanted to major in English. My father didn't say a word when I told him. Too proud to yell, he just went a little stiffer. We both hated scenes and between us normal conversation was impossible; with my father, it was either silence or a furious debate.

Anyway, we both knew he wasn't delighted with me, and I didn't need to be told why. He was a self-made success, having gone into lawn furniture just in time for the suburban land rush after the War. Suddenly everybody needed red maples and patio chaises. There was this young lawyer, Steve, only a few years out of school but already with a mortgage, wife, and son. My father knew his uncle, so he threw a little work his way. I can see how the two of them would have hit it off. Maybe I was even a little jealous of him; there isn't much logic to jealousy. Out of the blue Steve called me up over Christmas vacation and invited me to have lunch with him at a fancy restaurant. It wasn't hard to figure out what was up. "I ran into Steve," Dad said with ponderous nonchalance when he got home that night. "Said he asked you to lunch. Nice of him." So I went. I thought that having disappointed my father in the monumental, I could afford to oblige him in the trivial.

We met at the office Steve shared with two other attorneys, one of whom later became a famous union-buster. Pictures of Steve's wife and son were the first thing I noticed. There was not only the usual diptych on his desk but three others hung around the room. In the yard, on vacation, under the Christmas tree. No family man could be a shyster. Steve's hair was newly cut and his shirt terribly white. I remember how he lounged behind his big desk and took out a fifty-cent piece. Even then you hardly ever saw one and I wondered if he'd gotten it especially for the occasion. He held the coin up between his finger and thumb and said, "You won't have two of these to rub together." I laughed at him, of course; it was all so clumsily miscalculated. And yet, four years later, I wound up going into the business anyway.

I spent a couple years on the road selling before I got an office job. Already foreign competition was sending business down the chute. A couple years later Dad sold out. But he had me written into the deal. You want my factory, my stock, my good will, you take my son. Margot had been born by then and I too had a mortgage. So I stayed in an office job. The new owners, shrewd, wise Armenians, branched out and survived. They tolerated, then got used to me. No lucky/unlucky escape into insecurity for me.

It took my son's self-exile in a bathroom to remind me how bored I am by my work. And the truth is I've never even been much good at it.

Tonight, I was inching home in the usual traffic jam when I was seized by this overwhelming desire to see Victor, not to talk to him, but literally *to lay my eyes on him*. This must have been what my wife had felt that first Sunday. The sun was going down fast when I got home but I went straight from the garage to the Hoffmans and borrowed their ladder. I had to see Victor. I couldn't wait. My wife saw me from the kitchen and came outside. She was alarmed. "What are you going to do?" she cried. Margot was upstairs packing. She'd been doing it all week.

I laid the ladder carefully against the side of the house, just beside the bathroom window. It was a sultry August night and I could see the window was open. I didn't want to frighten Victor, to make him think he was under assault. I tried to keep from breathing too loudly or scraping the ladder against the wall.

I climbed slowly upward, sweating. I still had my tie and jacket on. The setting sun turned the white shingles red and orange. I hadn't considered it before, but my son's one view was due west.

I looked down and there was my wife, her hands clasped together as if in exasperated prayer. She did not look up at me. I could see the gray in her hair. We hardly ever watched television together anymore. I was always reading in the evenings, trying to keep up with Victor. We had never even looked at the slides from France. What did she do while I was wandering along the Nevsky Prospect? Talk to her friends on the phone? Copy out new recipes? Fret about the family? Curse the bargain she had made? Check the want-ads?

From Margot's room I could hear the unpleasant sound of hangers being scraped along the metal rod in her closet. The Hoffmans were barbecuing and the air stank of chicken fat. The higher I climbed the less quickly the sun seemed to be going down. Nevertheless, the days were growing shorter. The maple tree at the end of the yard already had a few red leaves on top.

To peer in the bathroom window, I had to stand on the next to last rung and lean over to the right. It was dangerous but I didn't care. I had to see my son. To see him.

There he was, sitting in nothing but a pair of underpants on the toilet seat, bent over the book in his lap with his feet resting on the side of the tub so that he looked as small, curled up, and self-contained as a snail. I must have blocked his light because he glanced up and saw me. I nearly fell and, if my son hadn't smiled so sweetly at me, I probably would have.

Imaginary Epilogue

Victor comes out tomorrow morning. On Labor Day we drive Margot up to college and Victor says he'd love to come. Margot rids herself of us as quickly as she can, but not without kisses all around. Victor starts school the next day and I go back to work. My wife becomes happier or at least more tranquil. We begin watching a little television together in the evenings while Victor does his homework and reads. My erotic dreams finally cease. On Saturday we invite the Hoffmans over for dinner and show them the slides of our trip to France.

Mrs. Podolski Defines *Schlimmbesserung*

"My dear, how kind. Soup's just the thing but could you put it in the"—cough, cough—"refrigerator? Not very hungry. I'll save it for later."

After a week of persistent bronchitis, my friend Mrs. Podolski was not looking tip-top and it seemed to me her customary ursine vitality had shrunk to a sparrow's. After letting me in, she tottered into the living room and to her favorite chair, a colossal thing of brown leather with arms like planks and a table-sized ottoman. She dropped into it like a lump of lead into a lake of molasses and there were three more coughs. On the chair's left arm a thin paperback lay splayed on top of the black remotes. She noticed my alarm and made a joke—her kind of joke.

"Illnesses are a bit like vacations, my dear. As a rule, it's just the last one you don't come back from."

Mrs. Podolski often ripped off these impromptu epigrams. Since I couldn't think how to respond to this one, and it didn't call for a reply anyway, I fell back on convention.

"What's the doctor say?"

She fluttered her hand. "Oh, what do they always say? Be patient and take your medicine. Words to live by. . . . But tell me, what's new with you? How are things at work?

I sighed. "Trying."

"Oh?"

"New software," I whined.

“You don’t like it?”

“Everybody hates it. It’s a catastrophe. More glitches than—” Unable to come up with a decent simile I trailed off, “Too many glitches. You know.”

Mrs. Podolski coughed, smiled, nodded, coughed. “*Schlimmbesserung*,” she said, finally.

For a moment I thought she might be clearing her throat. “Pardon?”

“Quite a useful German word.”

“But a mouthful.”

“My friend Gerhard used to say, ‘We Teutons don’t have long words, just small ones we like to smash together.’ Take *Freundschaftsbezeigungen, for instance, which nicely describes that soup you toted all the way over here.”*

“It doesn’t mean chicken soup, does it?”

“Not even close,” she chortled. Mrs. P. laughed a lot, yet never in the way you expect a seventy-nine-year-old widow to do, not even when she had bronchitis. “No, my dear. I’m pretty sure that would be Hühnersuppe. Freundschaftsbezeigungen means something like a demonstration of friendship.”

“How about that other word? The Schlimm thingee.”

“Schlimmbesserung. As I say, it fits your office’s new software. Fits rather perfectly, in fact.” She picked up the paperback and showed me the cover. The Marquise of O— by Heinrich von Kleist.

“I don’t know it.”

“Kleist was good, a genius, poor fellow. Couldn’t get settled in life. He kept trying to make his life better until he blew his brains out at thirty-four. It’s because of him that I thought of Schlimmbesserung.”

"Which means?"

"Schlimm means worse and besserung improvement. See? Smash. Think about it."

I did. "Oh. Got it. It means improving things in a way that makes them worse, right?"

"Worse, yes."

"So, Kleist's improvements to his life led to suicide?"

"I suppose you could say so. The Kleists were an old Prussian military family and went on being one. A Kleist led the panzers into France. Heinrich renounced his commission when he was a teenager then enrolled in a university to study science and turn himself into a man of the Enlightenment. Then he read Kant and, for some reason, that changed his mind. He dumped math for writing—journalism, stories, and especially plays. Lebensplan nach lebensplan. One of his ideas was to get married and another to assassinate Napoleon. . . . But it wasn't Kleist's restless, unhappy life that made me think of *Schlimmbesserung*. In fact, I only just saw how well it suits him personally. No, according to the pedant who wrote the introduction to this book of stories, the word was dreamed up by a wit to describe what a clutzy editor did to one of Kleist's plays. The moron thought he'd improve Kleist's language and, well—*Schlimmbesserung*. Look, my dear, talking to you seems to have given me an appetite." Cough, cough. "I think I might do with a bit of that soup, after all."

"Good!"

I leapt from the couch and bounded into the kitchen. While I was heating up the soup Mrs. Podolski called in to me, suggesting a game. Mrs. P. is very fond of games.

"We'll call it the *Schlimmbesserung* Game. I name something new that's worse than what it's supposed to be better than. Then you do the same. First one to run out of ideas loses—unless we're still going when the soup's ready; then it's a dead heat."

I was glad to hear that her voice sounded stronger. "You're on. You lead off."

"Well, I can't use new *software*, of course. How about the new *management*? You know, the kind that's going to centralize everything so as to be much more *efficient*."

"Spot on. Okay, my turn. Let's see. How about the new *diet*?"

"Good one, my dear. Soy milk and rice cakes. Red meat and raw kale."

"For instance."

"All right. The new *husband*."

"New husbands aren't always worse than old ones, are they?"

"True. But often enough. Take it from me, dear."

"Okay. The new *constitution*. Like when there's a military coup or a bunch of theocrats win an election?"

"I'll accept it. How about the new prayer book—no, the new Bible!"

"As in *see in a mirror dimly* rather than *through a glass darkly*?"

"And so on."

"New *prices*."

"Yup. Always higher. The new *music*."

"The new *supermarket*."

"The new *doctor*."

"The new *bridgework*."

"The new *traffic pattern.*"

"New skyline?"

"Thinking of that hideous pile that looks like it survived Hiroshima?"

"That's the one."

"Righto. Okay, the new *blue jeans.*"

"Those really tight ones I keep seeing and that you don't go in for?"

"Yes. *Those.*"

"The new *hairstyle.*"

"The new *reality show.*"

"The whole new television *season*!"

"The *new journalism.*"

"The New Left—*and* the New Right, too."

By now we were giggling like teenagers. "The new *math*!" I shouted.

"The new *New Wave*!"

"New *Coke*!"

Mrs. P. paused but I encouraged her, "Come on. You're not stumped, are you?"

"Just thinking, my dear. Okay, the new *thinking.*"

"Ha! The new *tax code.*"

"The new *grammar.*"

"The new *black.*"

"The new little black *dress.*"

Mrs. Podolski hesitated and I shouted, “Bingo! Soup’s on. Let’s call it a tie.”

She groaned as she pulled herself out of her chair and coughed deeply three times before grimly grumbling, “The *new normal*.”

Mrs. Podolski on Forgiveness

We first met in the local Walgreens late on a February afternoon. The snow from the week before, dirty now, was still piled up alongside sidewalks and streets. An even bigger storm was forecast to blow in from the west that night. I was nearly out of tampons, toothpaste, fluid for my contacts, and I needed a new shower cap, having already stapled the old one twice to make it tight.

When I arrived at the drug store, small flakes had just begun drifting down. I took a basket and foraged through the shelves. There was a long line at the prescription counter at the end of which was an elderly lady with a cane. Her stolidity drew my eye, and something about her face. She was wearing a woolen overcoat with a fur collar, the kind you never see anymore. The woman didn't look at all frail; on the contrary, she made me think of a mother bear.

I could have gone to the front counter with my purchases but instead I took my place behind this imposing, queenly, old lady. I noted that she wasn't so much leaning on her cane as gripping it like a potential weapon.

The line wasn't moving. A heavy-set bald man in a Patriots parka was squabbling with the pharmacist. A mother with a whining boy left the line, swearing. People craned their necks and muttered.

My mother bear turned her head. She had lively blue eyes. "According to Saint Augustine," she whispered, "patience is the companion of wisdom." This was my first experience of Mrs. Podolski's odd, random autodidact's erudition. I took it as a challenge.

"Mary Gordon wrote that waiting's the vocation of the dispossessed."

She turned around and gave me a warm smile, her face beaming with delight. "I liked *Final Payments* and *The Shadow Man*, too."

I said I'd read the first but not the second.

"You should." She sighed. "And so, we wait."

I resumed the game. "Fran Lebowitz said the opposite of talking isn't listening but waiting."

"So true. And so nice to talk."

I looked over my shoulder at the window at the front of the store. The storm had arrived early. Snow was coming down like white drapes blown around when somebody forgot to shut the windows.

"Did you drive?" I asked.

"Since my last accident, I hardly drive at all," she said rather merrily.

"Let me walk you home. It's getting bad out. I'll worry if you don't."

She agreed and we exchanged names.

She eventually picked up her medicine then we walked the three blocks to her apartment building. She invited me in, introduced me to Maraska slivovitz, and I stayed for lasagna and a salad. She had a lot to say to me about a lot of things. Since then, I've visited Mrs. Podolski at least once every week.

That was four years ago, when I was twenty-two, just a year out of college where I'd majored in English. As I didn't want to go to graduate school, let alone back home, and needed an income, I trained as a paralegal. I had just taken up my first job.

I relish the astonishing monologues of this wise widow and retired nurse, even the ones that feel interminable, even the most cutting. "After they put in a few years," she told me, "nurses are tough as an old bull whip—and can be used like one, too." She has plenty of friends but none who were prepared, like me, to listen to what they dismiss as her rambling.

"They prefer talking about grandchildren and TV to listening to me. They're all too old."

I fill two needs for Mrs. Podolski: for an audience and contact with a younger generation. She's a great, garrulous friend who's introduced me to a lot more than good plum brandy. It was as if she had been corked up since her husband died and has been effervescing since the cork came out on that snowy afternoon in Walgreens.

Like many English majors, I'm a poète manqué. I wrote a lot of bad poems in college and had two in the literary magazine. I was the only contributor who wasn't also on the staff—but I gave up writing after graduation. It was Mrs. Podolski who made me take it up again. I began making poems by recreating and compressing our conversations, which is to say her monologues. Here's the first one I wrote. It will give you an idea of my versifying and Mrs. Podolski's ironic way of talking to me.

While we were finishing the dishes
Mrs. Podolski began to talk
in that facetious way of hers
about what she calls "my wishes
for you, dear." In this fairy tale I walk
through a life Croesus couldn't afford
sealed off from its chills by thick furs,
immunized, triumphant, and adored.

She doesn't really mean it, doesn't
want me to think she does; she'd despise

anyone like that even if it wasn't
me but de Beauvoir or Curie, bent
under the weight of a Nobel prize,
fawned on by the Nordic King and Queen.
No, it wasn't at all what she meant
but precisely what she didn't mean.

Last Sunday, Mrs. P. began a long riff that I've tried to reproduce rather than versify. The proximate cause of her homily was something I said. I was describing the comportment of a divorcing couple I'd observed at work while taking notes on negotiations. The husband accepted all the demands of his unfaithful wife then announced that he forgave her. To me, he looked calm, at peace, not happy but resigned to the end of the marriage. When he said he'd forgiven her, the wife, a nervous woman with a pretty face, paled and reached for a tissue.

I said, "He was better off than she was. It was obvious."

That set Mrs. Podolski off. I said hardly anything but took mental shorthand of what follows, because—for writers at least—writing is the opposite of talking.

You think the forgiver gains more than the forgiven? My dear, I believe you're right. The guilty can go on feeling guilty while forgiving neutralizes resentment and frees all those nasty ions of vengefulness. It can work even if you're just pretending.

A couple months ago, Mrs. Debeque confessed that she'd called me an insufferable know-it-all during an afternoon of canasta with Mrs. Ardekian and Mrs. Gutman. Afterwards, she realized it would get back to me before the sun was down, as it did. She phoned to say she was terribly sorry and didn't really mean it and, well, there was wine. Of course, I forgave her. I even said I didn't disagree with what she said. Yes, you laugh. Maybe you don't disagree either? Anyway, now I'm at ease with Mrs. D. while she can't look me in the face.

Then there's what happens if you *don't* forgive. Gert Talonsky won't let go of a betrayal half a century old, a boyfriend stolen in eleventh grade. She hugs that old resentment to her withered breast like a new puppy. I've heard the story a dozen times. It's no wonder she suffers from reflux. I doubt the friend who swiped the boy remembers it, let alone the boy, if either of them is still alive.

You know I was raised Catholic. The Church may have co-opted sex, tortured so-called heretics, and terrorized the faithful with the threat of frightful after-lives, but in return it offered forgiveness—confession, penance, ways to wipe the slate clean. And, if all else failed, there was the intercession of a mommy to whom daddy had to listen. That's why there are so many Notre Dames of this and thats. The BVM wasn't the kind of mother who says wait till your father gets home. There was nothing she couldn't forgive.

Every Saturday, I had to traipse to Saint Barnabas and climb up to that little booth with its grill and wireless line to God. It wasn't so bad when Father Joe was the operator, much worse if it was Father Jankowski. Joe liked kids and favored a handful of Hail Marys; Father Jankowski saw everybody under eighteen as sinful vipers and routinely handed out a dozen novenas. Good cop, bad cop. I hated confession yet I liked being officially forgiven. You know that feeling you get after the dentist's through with you, that sense of invulnerability? That's what it was like for me for a couple of hours on Saturday afternoons.

What? Oh yes, *indulgences*. Just the objection an ex-Protestant *would* offer a lapsed Catholic. Do you know much about indulgences, my dear? No? Just the Tetzel-Luther business? Well, there's a whole history of indulgences.

Forgiveness, like any asset, has to come from somewhere. Indulgences were a kind of banking. The Church taught that the withdrawals came from this thing called the Treasury of Merit. The depositors were the saints and martyrs and the BVM. The biggest was Jesus, of course. An indulgence was a loan or mortgage that had to be repaid by penances prescribed by ordained priests. It was usually money or land, capital for all those medieval lazar houses, orphanages, and crusades. Between the Treasury of Merit and owning the Keys to the Kingdom, the Church was well set up to dispense forgiveness and, in the fullness of time, to be thoroughly corrupted. Tetzel, though, was different. He interested me. I read what I could about him and, in my opinion, the man was a pathetic figure, a dutiful fool.

Tetzel was a Dominican, a popular preacher who rose to be Inquisitor in Poland and then in Saxony, Luther's stomping ground. I think Brother Tetzel believed all he did was in accord with Church doctrine. He was an insurance salesman who didn't own the company or write its policies but excelled at selling them. He sermonized, recommending his wares to potential buyers by appealing in the voices of their sinful parents suffering the pains of Purgatory. People forget that.

Imagine the pitch. Bargain-priced forgiveness from a friar and inquisitor, authorized by the Pope himself in Rome. Gutenberg's contraption mass produced the little tickets as it later did Luther's *Theses*. Bestsellers all. Heaven knows how many indulgences Tetzel sold, but we do know that one-third of all books bought in Germany in those days were by Martin Luther. Funny, no? Well, doesn't new technology always give and take away?

But back to our indulgences, my dear. If people would shell out to save a dead parent, why not a live son or daughter, a wife or husband? Why not *oneself*? Who'd know better what needed to be forgiven? And beyond past sins, why not buy forgiveness in advance especially if, as the chief Father of the Church laid down, we were predestined to commit them? It's no wonder that when Tetzel's cavalcade pulled into town it felt like a visit from the heavenly host.

Luther may or may not have nailed those theses to the church door in Wittenberg. I've always thought the story too good to be true. I do know that he sent them to the Archbishop of Brandenburg. Turns out that Archbishop Albert bought his post with money borrowed from earthly bankers. The Fuggers didn't issue indulgences; they had to be paid. So, Albert needed cash, just as Leo did for fixing up Saint Peter's. The two made a deal to split the money collected by Tetzel. There's no evidence Tetzel ever took a pfennig for himself, making him a bigger dupe than any of his customers.

It's never good to mix forgiveness up with money; Luther was certainly right about that. And my favorite story about Tetzel is a good illustration. It may be no truer than the one about nailing the theses to the church door. Luther did spread the tale, just as he quoted Tetzel's infamous jingle.

When the gold in the casket rings,

The rescued soul toward Heaven springs.

Luther painted Tetzel as a money-grubbing con man; but the story shows him as ridiculous, not dishonest, which was probably more devastating.

Who's a more ambiguous figure than Luther with his constipation and his courage? He aroused the peasants to demand justice then called for their massacre. He inspired the iconoclasts and preached against them for a week. He opposed the Church's tyranny but championed serfdom. He extolled Christian love and railed against Jews like a Sturmfuhrer.

When Luther learned that Tetzel was dying, he took up his pen again. He was two-faced here as well. Luther composed two things. One was a touching private letter of consolation to his old adversary; the other was this story which he published.

Luther set his story in 1517, the year of the *Theses*. An impoverished knight had borrowed large sums from the local Cistercians. The monks refused to forgive the debt. This knight happened to be in Juterbog when Tetzel's parade arrived to the customary acclaim. He listened to the sales-pitch and watched the money pour into the oak caskets. After Tetzel left the town to make his way to Zinna, the knight waylaid the procession and stole the caskets. Enraged, Tetzel shook his fist and bellowed that for this great sin the knight would be damned through all eternity. The knight raised his visor and laughed as Tetzel recognized the man to whom he had just sold, for fifty guilders, an indulgence for the future sin of robbery.

What do you think, my dear? Isn't the vacuum of forgetting preferable to the condescension of forgiving? The first can be relied on, the second is uncertain.

Back to Brother Tetzel. The Church condemned him. Later, it pardoned him but, of course, he was never forgiven. That thieving knight may have gone to Hell, but it's the misguided, hard-working, faithful Tetzel history has damned.

The indulgence racket cost the Church half of Europe. I'm sure remission without punishment gave license to those who like getting away with things; but I imagine that, for the principled and guilt-ridden, indulgences weren't enough. My brother Stan was like that.

One winter evening when we were kids, my mother told me to call him in for dinner. Stan was outside with his friends, sledding and tossing snowballs. Dusk was just turning into night. I went to the door and, coming from the lighted kitchen, couldn't see anything. I called Stan, but he didn't answer. I hollered for him twice more. His friends booed. Stan saw me lit up in the doorway. He didn't want to come in. His friends would make fun of him if he did. So, he threw a snowball at me. More like an iceball, really. It hit me square in the face. His pals cheered. My nose bled.

Stan was torn, proud of his great throw but horrified too. My father saw the blood coming from my nose, yelled at Stan to come in right away and he did. When he saw the blood on my face his own went white.

"Punish me!" he demanded.

My mother, washing my face, said it was just an accident, that she knew Stan didn't mean it, that it was all right. She told him to go wash his hands and come to the table.

Stan began to cry. "No!" he insisted. "I *aimed*. Punish me!"

"Go to your room," Father said. "No dinner for you tonight." He didn't say it loudly or angrily but almost tenderly. *Tenderly*, that's close to one of the original meanings of indulgence.

I remember Stan running up the stairs that night as fast as he ran down them on Christmas morning.

The End of the War

By the ninth year we believed it might never end and gave up trying to win it because trying to win a war is the surest way to make it go on; that is, when you try to win a war it's only the war that wins. This was the sum of the wisdom we had achieved in nearly a decade; in fact, it was the solitary thing we had achieved in all those years of fighting and suffering. Now that we were pushing thirty, we couldn't bear that the war would go on and on, not just for another decade but for the rest of our lives. Nevertheless, simply laying down our arms and surrendering would be futile because of the swarms of gung-ho seventeen- and eighteen-year-olds, weaned on tales of glory and revenge, who wouldn't think of giving up, at least not for another nine more years. As for ourselves, our generation, we reckoned that it wasn't the enemy that needed to be defeated but the war itself. It had already ruined everything it touched, from dairy farms to post-adolescence, from stone bridges to summer romances, from highway overpasses to bedside manners, from the pride of old men to the breasts of pubescent girls. So, by and by, we came up with a plan, desperate yet not inelegant. A dozen of us decided to organize a theater festival, as we announced, *right on the front lines* (of which there really weren't any), *right in the middle of the battlefield* (though there really was no field). Our great production would stretch from the trenches to the rear echelons, from the barracks all the way to the field kitchens and mobile hospitals. We persuaded ourselves that in this way we might bamboozle the war into thinking it wasn't a real war at all but only make-pretend. Our theatrics would confuse the generals, baffle the colonels, mystify the majors, deceive even the sergeants (who are always the most difficult to fool). We would make them believe they were not combatants at all but directors, stagehands, managers, grips, prop men, script girls, even, in the case of the elderly and august field marshal who headed the General Staff, a playwright. When the last scene of the final act was played, we would invite the international press and hand out awards. Critics from all the papers and television networks, bored with repeating patently false government communiqués, would be eager for the novelty of the business, and also frightened of missing something so unheard-of, so *avant-garde*, that they would flock to our vast theater. We would work the artillery barrages into the script, and the nighttime bombings as well. The streams of refugees would serve as extras in our epic production. We would take pains that even the smallest skirmish was properly lit, that there would be plenty of applause for heroes who acted persuasively heroic and no less for cowards capable of acting convincingly craven. If the cowards should turn out to be the more persuasive, then the cowards would receive the acting award and not the heroes. And soon, the war would forget its intention to be endless; it would be gobbled up by the glory of art as, under our high-school microscopes, we'd watched a paramecium ingest some morsel that became a piece of satisfied paramecium paddling purposefully through its little world. In this way, so we thought, the war too would gradually cease to be itself and become the subject of our vast theater-piece complete with its rising action, its recognition, reversal, and climax, with its rapidly falling action concluding in a most delicious dénouement where each enmity and conflict would be unknotted and made smooth, when all the terrible energies of our sanguinary youth would at last come to rest. The audience of millions would feel this approaching closure like a train rumbling toward the platform and this rumbling, this muted expectancy would be satisfied even if one didn't particularly care for the play (it's true that most people don't like most plays) because everyone would know that soon they would be permitted to rise from their narrow seats (there is never enough leg room for those who have legs), released and granted all the time they wanted to mull over the faults of the drama in a café, then to make their way home, climb between clean sheets, and forget all about it.

www.ingramcontent.com/pod-product-compliance
Lightning Source LLC
LaVergne TN
LVHW041034150826
845672LV00001B/311

* 9 7 8 9 3 6 3 5 4 2 4 0 2 *